ALSO BY JACQUELINE WOODSON

JACQUELINE WOODSON

REMEMBER US

 Nancy Paulsen Books

NANCY PAULSEN BOOKS

An imprint of Penguin Random House LLC, New York

First published in the United States of America by Nancy Paulsen Books,
an imprint of Penguin Random House LLC, 2023

Copyright © 2023 by Jacqueline Woodson

Visit us online at PenguinRandomHouse.com.

Library of Congress Cataloging-in-Publication Data
Names: Woodson, Jacqueline, author.
Title: Remember us / Jacqueline Woodson.
Description: New York: Nancy Paulsen Books, 2023. | Summary: "The summer before seventh grade,
as the constant threat of housefires looms over her Brooklyn neighborhood, basketball-loving Sage is
trying to figure out her place in her circle of friends, when a new kid named Freddy moves in"
—Provided by publisher.
Identifiers: LCCN 2023009347 | ISBN 9780399545467 (hardcover) | ISBN 9780399545481 (ebook)
Subjects: CYAC: Friendship—Fiction. | Basketball—Fiction. | Bushwick (New York, N.Y.)—Fiction. |
African Americans—Fiction. | LCGFT: Novels.
Classification: LCC PZ7.W868 Re 2023 | DDC [Fic]—dc23
LC record available at https://lccn.loc.gov/2023009347
Printed in the United States of America
ISBN 9780399545467
1st Printing

LSCH

Edited by Nancy Paulsen
Design by Marikka Tamura
Text set in Maxime Pro

For Kwame & Jason,
brothers from other mothers

After the year of fire
vines rise up
through the rest of our lives
of smoke
of flame
of memory.
As if to say
We're still here.
As if to say
Remember us.

1

THE MOON IS BRIGHT TONIGHT. And full. Hanging low above the house across the street where an orange curtain blows in and out of my neighbors' window. Out and in. And past the curtain there's the golden light of their living room lamps. Beyond that, there is the pulsing blue of their television screen. I see this all now. I see a world continuing.

And in the orange and gold and blue I'm reminded again of the year when sirens screamed through my old neighborhood and smoke always seemed to be billowing. Somewhere.

That year, from the moment we stepped out of our houses in the morning till late into the night, we heard the sirens. Down Knickerbocker. Up Madison. Across Cornelia. *Both* ways on Gates Avenue. Down Ridgewood Place. Rounding the corners of Putnam, Wilson, Evergreen . . .

Evergreen. Sometimes a word comes to you after time has passed. And it catches you off guard. *Evergreen.* The name of a family of trees. And the name of a block in Brooklyn. Evergreen. Another way of saying *forever*.

That year, nothing felt evergreen.

Palmetto. A word that has never left me. A word that in my mind is evergreen. *Palmetto.* The name for both a stunning tree and an oversize cockroach. Palmetto was also the name of a street in my old neighborhood. And that year, Palmetto Street was burning.

2

THAT WAS THE YEAR WHEN, one by one, the buildings on Palmetto melted into a mass of rock and ash and crumbled plaster until just a few walls were left standing. Walls that we threw our balls against and chased each other around. And at the end of the day, when we were too tired to play anymore, they were the walls we simply sat down by and pressed our backs into, staring out over a block that was already, even as we stared at it with our lips slightly parted and our hands shielding the last of the sun from our eyes, almost gone.

We said *Well, nothing lasts for always, right?*

We said *One day even the whole earth will disappear.*

We were just some kids making believe we understood.

But we didn't. Not yet.

We didn't understand the fires. Or life. Or the world.

But we knew that neighborhood *was* our world.

And we knew . . . our world was burning.

3

THAT WAS THE YEAR OF Freddy too.

4

FREDDY MOVED INTO THE CORNER building on Palmetto Street right where it was sliced through by a small block called Ridgewood Place. The brick houses on Ridgewood Place felt like they came from another time. Each house was just as perfect as the one beside it. The cars parked out in front of the houses were undented and shining. We didn't understand how the people who lived on Ridgewood Place got such nice houses and fancy cars. But we understood why their brick houses remained standing long after the wooden houses of Palmetto Street had burned to the ground. So we slitted our eyes as we walked past the houses on Ridgewood Place, jealous because the kids who lived inside that brick didn't have to worry about how quickly flames flew. And we slitted our eyes because we knew they didn't have to sleep with their robes and shoes at the foot of their beds. We knew if those kids woke up in the middle of the night, it was only to go to the bathroom or climb into their parents' bed during a thunderstorm.

5

HEY, GIRL!

The first time I ever talked to Freddy was the day he called to me from his window. I had been dribbling my basketball through my legs as I walked up the block but stopped to see who was yelling. It was summer, and the one tree on Palmetto Street was in front of his building. That's what I remember now—looking up at Freddy through all that green.

Hey, yourself, I yelled back.

Where's the park at?

What park?

My dad said there was a park around here somewhere. With hoops.

I shrugged. *I don't know anything about some park,* I said.

But you got a ball.

So?

A hot wind came out of nowhere and trembled the leaves. I didn't want to be yelling in the street up at some kid's window, and something about that wind made me feel a way. So I gave a little wave and then broke into a jog toward the park.

6

FREDDY SHOWED UP AT THE basketball courts the next day anyway. We eyed each other. He was a little shorter than me and skinny. He was light-skinned, with a short messy afro that needed an afro pick, and his eyes kept changing colors depending on how the sun hit them—first the darkest blue I'd ever seen, then gray, then that darkest blue again.

Thought you didn't know where the park was at, he said.

I shrugged. *You found it anyway, so no big deal.*

Who got next? he asked.

I said *What's your name?*

Freddy, he said. *I just moved to Palmetto Street.*

You got next now, I guess, Freddy from Palmetto Street.

A guy from the other team said *That block is burning down, son.*

Who's doing it? Freddy asked.

Who knows? the guy said back. *Something. Or* somebody.

Well, not my house, Freddy said.

Everywhere, I said. *The whole neighborhood. But mostly your block.*

Not my house, Freddy said again. He looked off then. Toward the sound of the sirens. Toward Palmetto Street.

We were playing two-on-two. Me and this guy named Randy and two guys from Putnam Avenue who thought they had game but didn't. Me and Randy were winning. I had been playing ball since I was a little kid. My mother said the minute I could hold a ball with two hands, I was looking for a game. Most days the only place I wanted to be was on the basketball court.

I dribbled the ball. Shot it. Watched it sink into the basket. A guy on the other team cursed. Randy slapped my hand. Said *Nice shot, Sage.*

I was the only girl on the court. Always. The only girl in a basketball shirt and high-tops. The only girl who pulled her hair back into a braid every day of every year no matter what. And one of the best players in the park. The guys who played there regularly knew me and always chose me first when they were putting teams together. Basketball was the thing I loved most in the world. More than candy or cartoons. More than roller-skating or roller coasters. I felt ball in every part of my body—my feet, my knees, my hands and arms. My head too. How many times had I gotten into trouble for sitting in class imagining a slam dunk or a stutter-step dribble around a player to the basket, score! Too many.

All I wanted was to be around anybody who wanted to talk about Bob McAdoo joining the Knicks and Kareem Abdul-Jabbar leaving the Bucks for the Lakers or who had the most points in a game in history.

Wilt Chamberlain, Freddy said that afternoon. *A hundred points in 1962.*

Yeah, but against what team? I asked.

Knicks, he said. *Of course. Who else would let a brother score on them like that?*

Watch out, Randy said. *Sage is a Knicks fan!*

Me too, Freddy said. *Wilt still put a beating on them, though. Warriors were hot that year.*

Randy shot a jumper that ended the game. He slapped my palm, and Freddy asked the two guys we'd just beat if either of them wanted to be on his team.

I'm hungry. I'm out, one of the guys said. We all held out our hands for him to slap, and then he was jogging across the park.

I'm in, the other guy said.

Then we were back to playing. Freddy took an outside shot and missed. I grabbed the rebound. Passed it to Randy. Randy was thirteen but not that tall and was about to head off on a full ride to a boarding school in Massachusetts. He'd be leaving in the fall.

You ever been to a real game? I asked Freddy when we took a water break.

He shook his head. *You?*

Nah.

That day, I didn't tell Freddy the rest. That my dad had planned to take me to a real game when I was older. That he said *Keep playing. Maybe I'll be coming to see you on the court someday.*

That was a long time ago.

I took a long gulp of water, blinking back memories of my dad while my head was down. Then I picked up the ball and started dribbling hard—around the back, through my legs. I spun it up on my pointer, jumped it to my middle finger, then back again.

Y'all ready? I asked.

The others nodded. Randy grabbed the ball, sprinted back over to the hoop, took a layup, and sunk it.

Like always, a group of little kids and some old neighborhood dudes had gathered to watch us. Every time I sank a shot, the little kids cheered.

You got your own fan club, Freddy said.

I'm that good, I said back.

We were still playing when the sun went down.

7

FOR A WHILE I HAD been best friends with a girl named Angie. Felt like one day we were all playing on the block together, letting our knees get scraped and clothes get dirty, next day, Angie was hanging with a group of girls who greased their hair into swirls against their foreheads, polished their nails, and brushed invisible dirt from their jeans.

We were all turning twelve that year, and everybody around me seemed to be noticing my clothes, my dirty sneakers, my messy braid and bitten-down nails.

Angie and I weren't enemies. But we weren't friends anymore either. She and the other girls had formed a small, tight circle.

With me on the outside of it.

8

EVERY MORNING, MY MOTHER LAID the *Daily News* out on our kitchen table and made me read it. I turned the pages slowly while I ate my bowl of cereal. One Saturday, as I was rushing through the paper so that I could head to the park to play ball, I saw the words *the Bushwick section of Brooklyn.*

We're in here! I said, my mouth filled with Frosted Flakes. *Bushwick's in the paper!*

I know, my mother said. *Keep reading.* She went over to the window and stared out at the green tops of the newly planted trees. Maybe she sighed, I don't remember now.

Because of the record number of buildings that have burned in this section of Brooklyn, I read out loud, *some have begun referring to Bushwick as The Matchbox.* I looked up from the paper.

The Matchbox?

My mother nodded. *I'm thinking it's time to move out of this neighborhood, Sage.*

But this was Daddy's house, I said. *He was a little boy here.*

I know.

He loved this place.

He did, my mother said. *But the neighborhood wasn't The Matchbox then.*

I looked down at the paper again.

They don't know anything, I said. *They don't live here. And how come they don't write about the good stuff? Like when we're having block parties and things like that? Or that time when Greg from down the block hit a baseball right out of the park and couldn't walk down the street without people coming out of their houses to pat him on the back. Remember how everyone was telling him he had a gift? You too. You said it.*

I was talking too fast. I knew it but couldn't stop. I didn't want to imagine living anywhere else. Yeah, I wanted to be safe. But I wanted to be safe *here.*

The fires are real, Sage.

They don't know us, I said again, and went back to the paper.

The story jumped to the next page, where there was a picture of a building on Palmetto Street in flames. Black smoke billowed out from the top-floor windows. I remembered that fire. I woke up to the sounds of sirens and my mother grabbing old blankets just as the sun was rising. I had wanted to go with her, to help whoever was getting burnt out. But it had been a weekday, just hours before I'd have to get up for school. My mother told me *Go back to sleep, Sage. I'll be home in a little while.*

So I did. Then, after school the next day, a bunch of us ran over to Palmetto. The first floor of that building was all that was left.

I don't want to move, I said, staring down at the newspaper. *I like it here.*

My mother turned and looked at me then. We had the same skin—dark brown and smooth. But our eyes were different. Hers slanted upward slightly, and her lashes were so long and straight, people asked if they were real. I had gotten my father's eyes. Regular eyes but with a dimple beneath the left one. That morning, my mother was wearing a red T-shirt with a picture of two skeletons and the words GRAND CANYON above them. She and my dad had gone there for their honeymoon.

A siren that started far away grew closer.

I know you worry about the fires catching up to us as much as I do, my mother said.

I ran my finger gently over the picture of the burning building. I remembered later that day, a kid who had lived in that building came to the park to play basketball. He and some of the other guys had been friends, and when he went to slap this guy named Al's palm, Al pulled him close.

You good, dude? Al asked. *Your people okay?*

The kid nodded, said *I don't want to talk about it. Everybody's fine, though. We staying with my aunt for now. She lives over in the Marcy Houses. Can I get in the game?*

His T-shirt and cutoffs were too big, but his sneakers looked brand new. I wondered if they'd lost everything in the fire.

Of course, bro, Al said.

That day we played three-on-two and two-on-two and one-on-one, but we made sure to keep the kid from Palmetto Street in the game. Somehow we knew, even though none of us had ever gotten burnt out, what a long and lonely walk it was back to his aunt's house. And we knew how ball made all the other stuff disappear.

I looked up at my mother. *You gonna find us a house made of brick?*

She nodded, came over to me, kissed the top of my head. *I'm gonna try. I wish you'd let me do something different with your hair,* she said, brushing stray hairs back with her hand.

It's fine like this.

I pulled my head away and tried to imagine a world where kids didn't get burnt out and I didn't have to sleep with a bathrobe at the foot of my bed. A world where sirens didn't scream deep into the night. A world where my mother didn't keep stacks and stacks of old blankets in the closet to help neighbors.

It'd be strange, I said. *To not think about . . . I mean, to not always worry about fires.*

I thought about Freddy in his top-floor apartment on Palmetto Street. And the baby that had just been born down the block. *But what about everyone else?* I asked. *They have to stay here.*

I'm sure lots of people in the neighborhood are making plans, Sage. If the fires don't force them out, the fear of fire might.

But what if the fire gets to them first?

Wish I knew how to answer that, my mother said.

I pulled the page with the burning building from the newspaper and folded it into an airplane. If my mother hadn't been there, I would have sailed it right out the window.

9

WHEN THE THING WE REMEMBER is gone, I wondered, what do we have left to remember it by?

So much I didn't remember about my father. But every day, I walked on the floors he had walked on, brushed my teeth in the sink he once brushed his teeth in. And every night, I lay in bed in a room that had been his as a boy and stared out the same window. From it, we'd seen the same stars.

10

I WAS BORN TWO DAYS after Thanksgiving just before the sun rose. I was named Sage by my mother. *Sage,* she said, *is a healing plant.* The smell of it was still in her nose when I came into the world. *I'd made the stuffing,* she said. *And maybe I'd used too much sage in it. But then you were here and the smell of it was everywhere. It was like it just settled all over you.*

I was born a Sagittarius. It's supposed to mean I'm wise. Energetic. Beyond my years. I don't know about any of that, but what I do know for sure is that Sagittarius is a fire sign.

And I was born a fireman's daughter.

Sage Michael Durham. The Michael was after my father.

Do you think about him all the time, Ma?

Day and night. And every time, I see him in the way you laugh.

Did he laugh a lot? I asked.

All the time, my mother said. *That man loved to laugh. And dream too. He grew up inside these walls, dreaming of becoming a fireman. And then . . . he did.*

And now the neighborhood my daddy loved so much was on fire.

11

WHEN PEOPLE ASK, I TELL them the truth. I remember bits and pieces of my father—his smile, his laugh. How tall he was and how big his hands were. I remember him cheering when I shot the ball into the kid-sized hoop and promising to take me to a Knicks game. I remember he liked pineapple juice and BBQ potato chips and his steak cooked medium rare. In the picture of him that I keep in my wallet, he's tall and dark and smiling. He's wearing a white undershirt and his fireman's pants with the red suspenders. He's holding his fireman's hat in his hands. If you look closely, you can see the dimple under his eye that's like mine. You can see the wedding band that my mother keeps in a box in her top drawer. You can see that my father had been here once. He had been alive—and laughing.

12

THAT YEAR, WE LEARNED THAT fire explodes through glass, melts siding, gobbles wood to gray ash. We stood in small, stunned crowds watching how it destroyed.

We watched the fires with our bandanas protecting our noses and mouths against the smoke and saw how quickly what once *was* a thing wasn't anymore.

Remember when Charlie lived there? we said to each other. *Isabel? Archie?*

And Freddy, who was still new to the neighborhood and didn't yet know, said *Just yesterday it wasn't like this.*

13

SO MANY NIGHTS MY MOTHER got to the fire before the firefighters did, bringing blankets with her. And sometimes water and food.

Drink something, she'd say to the people standing in shock outside their burning buildings.

She was there if someone needed soothing while they took their first deep gulps of smoke-free air.

She was there to hold them. And let them cry.

14

ONE AFTERNOON, WE WERE STANDING on Palmetto where two buildings were newly blackened, the roofs on both collapsed into the lower floors. On the street in front of the buildings, two cars had also burned. My mother said it had taken the firefighters hours and hours to get the fire under control and then more time to finally put it out. In the empty lot beside the burnt buildings, steam still rose from a charred mattress.

We gotta remember the once was, Freddy said softly, staring at what remained of the buildings.

We were standing in a small group—me, Freddy, Randy, and three other guys we'd been playing ball with. Me, Freddy, and Randy had been in the middle of crushing them when one of the guys said he was gonna go see if he could find anything where the new burnt buildings were. *Nobody's picked that spot yet,* he said. *It was still too hot this morning.*

So we'd all stopped playing ball and headed over.

What's the once was? I asked Freddy.

That's the once was, he said, pointing to the empty lot where buildings once stood. *From now on, we're always gonna be talking about what once was there. The buildings that are gone. They're . . . they're in the past now.*

I thought about my father. He, too, was a part of the *once was.* And soon I'd be part of the *once was* of Bushwick, of my block, of the park and the hundreds of basketball games I'd played there.

Something must have come over my face then, because Freddy touched my arm. *Hey. You good?*

I'm okay, I said.

Freddy and I stared at what remained of the buildings without saying anything else for a long time. The others had already left us and crossed the street to start looking for stuff, stepping carefully over wet, splintered wood. They pulled the front of their shirts over their noses to block the smell of smoke. The mist of the foam the firemen used to smother the flames still hung in the air.

Freddy and I finally pulled our own bandanas from where we'd tied them around our wrists and put them over our noses. As we headed into the lot, a little kid found a blackened Matchbox car, and we watched as he shouted and happy-danced around his friends, holding the treasure above his head like a trophy.

15

THE SUN BEAT DOWN ON Freddy and me as we bent over what was left of somebody else's life. We picked through glass and charred wood and pieces of plaster walls and stopped only to take long gulps of water from a fire hydrant that hadn't been all the way closed. The water was icy cold but tasted of metal and smoke.

I could hear some of the kids coughing a dry, raspy cough that I would later learn was the beginning of asthma.

Right near the hydrant, I found a melted picture frame. Inside, a mom stood smiling into the camera, holding twins in her arms. Behind her, the father looked down at the babies. The photo was blurred at the edges where water had gotten to it, making the whole family look like they were slowly being erased. I stared at the picture for a long time before laying it gently back down on a pile of crumbled plaster.

Then a little boy named Jacob, with the front of his raggedy gray sneaker flapping, ran over and found it. He grinned, and when he showed it to his friends, I could hear them oohing and aahing as they looked at the photo and Jacob held it, protective.

Cherishing a family he had probably never known.

16

HEY! FREDDY SAID, DIGGING SOMETHING black and wet from a small pool of water in the wreckage of the fire. *A wallet!* We stopped searching and picking and watched him slowly pull five soaking dollar bills from it.

Candy for everybody, he yelled. *My treat!*

Jacob ran to Freddy and hugged him hard. The other kids cheered. The search was over for now. We had found something amazing. A line of little kids skipped behind Freddy, all of them smiling. All of them already dreaming of candy buttons and Now & Laters, Milky Ways and Baby Ruths, licorice strings and Lemonheads.

Above us, the sun was still hot and bright. Jacob ran over to me and grabbed my hand.

He really gonna give us some? he asked worriedly. *He really gonna share?*

I nodded. Jacob had a front tooth missing and a small rip in his T-shirt. Maybe the shirt had been white at one time, but now it was yellowing and so short, his brown belly was exposed.

I like butterscotches, Jacob said. *You like butterscotches too?* Then he smiled up at me again.

I've forgotten so much about that year. But I have never forgotten Jacob.

17

MY MOTHER KEPT A BAG packed for each of us—clean underwear, toothbrush, and an outfit that she would change with the seasons. In her bag she also had some canned goods—corn, beans, SpaghettiOs, and sardines—and an envelope of fives and singles.

She checked extension cords, pressed her hand against walls when the smell of smoke was in the air.

It's not hot, she said.

The fire, she said, *isn't near.*

Still, at night I fell asleep to the symphony of sirens. Now close. Now far away again. Now loud. Now fading like a wailing baby who had finally been rocked to sleep.

18

I NEVER WAS FREE LIKE that, Freddy said one afternoon as we stopped down the block from his building to watch Jacob and some other little kids do flips on a half-burnt mattress. Weeks had passed since he'd bought us all candy with the money he'd found. And somewhere inside those passing weeks, we'd become friends. I'd even met his mom, who had a southern accent and Freddy's same eyes. It was true that Freddy loved basketball almost as much as I did, but we became friends for other reasons too. We were both only children. And maybe because of that, it was easy to be quiet with him. Or talk with him about everything. We knew the silence that came with being alone in our rooms, and we knew how good it felt to listen. And to be heard too.

Yeah you were, I said. *Every kid was free once. When I was little, I used to think I could fly. I'd jump off my couch with a towel tied around my neck. I wanted to be Superman.*

You mean Superwoman, Freddy said. *You would have been Superwoman. Or Supergirl.*

Nah, I wanted to be the strongest one, I said. *So that's Superman.*

Freddy had a small crease above his left eyebrow that got deep when he was thinking. *You know what's weird,* he said, the crease deepening. *Nobody's real. Not Superman or Supergirl or Superwoman.*

I know that.

So, Freddy said, *if it's all made up, how come Superman still gotta be the strongest? How come they can't all be the same amount of strong, right? Or what if Supergirl was the strongest?*

Right on! I shook my head. *It's like comic books got all this imagination but can't even imagine that.*

Yeah, Freddy said. *That's stupid.*

A fire truck moved slowly up Palmetto Street. The two men riding on the outside looked tired and grim, barely lifting their hands to wave. I watched them, wondering what fire they were coming from. What building was now a part of the *once was?* At the corner of Wyckoff Avenue, the truck made a left and disappeared. Across the street, a little boy sat on his mother's lap, still waving long after the fire truck was gone.

You're slick, Sage, Freddy said. *You got my brain thinking about stuff.* He smiled. *I see what you doing.*

All I said was I wanted to be the strongest one and that's Super-man.

Okay, Slick, Freddy said.

Okay, Slick, yourself.

Hey, Freddy! Sage! Jacob yelled. He was wearing bright green shorts and a T-shirt with a smiley face. *Watch me!* The other kids who had been jumping on the mattress with him were now circling it, watching him and waiting for their turn to jump on it alone.

Jacob did a standing backflip on the mattress, and the shorts became a green blur in the air. When he landed, he grinned over at us.

Now, that kid can fly, Freddy said as we both gave Jacob the thumbs-up.

You know what? I used to dream about flying too, Freddy continued, watching Jacob and the kids as he spoke. *When I was real little, I asked my mom when I was gonna grow wings. She looked at me like I was nuts. For some reason, I got it in my head that at some point all humans grew wings and flew.*

I laughed.

For real, Sage. It was the first time my uncle flew from New Orleans to visit us. And he told me when I was older, I could fly to see him. I didn't even make the connection to airplanes. I just thought that at some point everybody flew! When my mom told me he meant planes—and I realized I wasn't ever gonna grow wings—I was so mad!

Freddy looked at me. *See how slick you are. Got me remembering good stuff like that.*

I shrugged and went back to watching Jacob. Inside, though, I was smiling.

19

JACOB CANNONBALLED INTO THE SKY again. For a moment, gravity let him go and the grin on his face was as wide as the space between the hollowed-out buildings. But then he landed wrong and started screaming. The little kids around him raced off in every direction.

Freddy and I ran over to him, and he just lay there crying and holding his foot with both hands. I put my hand over his, asking him to let me see where it hurt. But he wouldn't take his hands away, so I just kept my hand on top of his, hoping it calmed him.

Don't tell my mama, Sage. Please don't tell my mama, he cried, his tears streaming down through the thin layer of dust that covered his small brown face. I knew he was worried because he and his friends weren't supposed to be playing in the burnt-out lots, but I just nodded. His ankle was starting to swell.

Jacob tried to sit up, gulping to catch his breath between sobs. Freddy helped him just as a woman in a headscarf and flip-flops ran toward us. She grabbed Jacob, lifting him into her arms. Jacob lay his head on her shoulder, his cries becoming a whimper as she soothed him. *You're okay, boo. Mommy's got you now. I'm here.*

He burrowed his head into her shoulder, and we watched her carry him out of the lot and down the block.

Then the other little kids, seeing that the coast was clear, ran back over to the mattresses and jumped and danced and spun on them as though nothing had happened. No fire. No Jacob landing wrong. No tears. They laughed and played like the memory was already gone from them. And maybe, for the time being, it was.

20

SOME DAYS THE FIRE TRUCKS arrived to false alarms, sirens growing louder as kids froze mid-hopscotch, one leg still bent above a number.

When the trucks were close enough to see, the tiniest kids on the block abandoned their playing and chased after them, frantically waving and yelling *Hey, Mr. Fireman! Mr. Fireman! Hey!* Their small hands and high voices pleading, as though to say *Please wave back. Please see me.*

Always, even when they looked tired as anything from rushing from fire to fire, the firemen waved back.

Some afternoons, as I sat on my basketball watching the waving children, I tried to imagine my father as a little boy. Did he chase fire trucks and shout *Hey, Mr. Fireman* too? Maybe the dream of being a fireman started for him way back when he was a tiny boy. Maybe the dream was inside every kid that ever ran after a wailing siren. Every kid that ever held their breath hoping, hoping, hoping a firefighter leaned off the side of the truck and waved back.

For a long time, my father had been the only Black firefighter in his squad. And lots of the white firefighters weren't kind. *They wouldn't speak to him,* my mother says. *Sent him into the most dangerous fires first.* But then he found his people. The year before I was born, my father joined the Vulcan Society—a fraternity of Black firefighters from all over the city. He transferred to Engine 234/Ladder 123 in Crown Heights, where there were other Vulcans. Still, in all the pictures, he's the tallest, the darkest, and the most handsome.

I could stare at pictures of him for hours. I liked seeing the features we shared—the dimple under our eye, the thick brows and dark eyes. And because he's looking directly into the camera in every single photo, it feels like he's looking at me. And smiling.

The year he died, the Vulcans came to his funeral. So many other firefighters too—a long line of them, straight-backed, their hats pressed to their chests as they walked slowly behind the pallbearers. After, when we all climbed into cars to head to the graveyard, the fire truck from my father's ladder company followed us, its siren whining long and low through the streets.

This memory, too, is evergreen.

21

THROUGH ALL THIS, AS THE fires burned, the brick buildings on Ridgewood Place kept standing. Some days we walked down the block dragging our hands along the bright blue and gold and black hoods of the fancy cars parked out in front of the houses. When curtains were pulled back, we glanced into the windows and saw glittering chandeliers. We saw pianos and television sets and thick, dark carpeting.

But it was Freddy who walked down that block every day on his way to meet us at the park. He knew more about the people living there than any of us did.

They have meat every night, he told us as we played ball. *Plus rice, greens, potatoes, corn. And dessert too. Red Jell-O. Lemon pudding.* Freddy said he passed by sometimes and the kids who lived in those houses were sitting on their stoops eating ice cream cones. *One time,* he said, *this little kid dropped his. He didn't even cry. Just ran inside. Two minutes later, boom! He's back outside with another one.*

That ice cream that he dropped? It just melted right on into the street, and none of them acted like they even cared. Freddy's blue-gray eyes slitted into remembering. *They acted like all the ice cream in the world was just inside their house, waiting for them. Wasn't even something special.*

As Freddy talked, we practiced our layups and outside shots and dribbled the ball through our legs and behind our backs. But all the while, our hearts singed with a jealous fire. We wanted what the kids on Ridgewood Place had. We wanted their couches, their ice cream cones, their red Jell-O and lemon pudding.

We wanted the permanence of their brick. The security of their stone.

22

LATE IN THE SUMMER, A yellow cab pulled up in front of Freddy's building. Freddy and I had been sitting on his stoop eating chocolate chip cookies his mother had made. She'd given us each four wrapped in a napkin, but she said the rest was for company and wouldn't tell us who the company was. But when a tall light-skinned man climbed out of the cab, Freddy jumped up so fast, he nearly dropped his cookies.

Uncle Angel! Freddy yelled, wrapping his arms around the man's waist. I'd never seen him so excited. I eyed the man he was hugging. He looked like Freddy's mother—same light brown skin, same reddish-brown hair and light eyes.

Then a pretty brown-skinned woman climbed out the back, holding a sleeping baby. She bent to kiss Freddy's forehead and smiled at me just as two kids climbed out of the cab and pushed past her and the baby to jump on Freddy and hug him. I sat there with my mouth open. I had never seen so much hugging and laughing in my life. The boy was about

Freddy's age, with the same eyes. Just as I was thinking this is the most blue-eyed Black people I'd ever seen in my life, a girl climbed out. She looked older than us and had brown eyes. Her reddish hair was pulled tight into long cornrows.

Sage, these my cousins! AndUncleAngelandAuntJasmine. And that's baby Paul asleep. Freddy was talking so fast and grinning so hard, I could barely understand what he was saying.

I waved, feeling shy suddenly.

That's Gwen and Shaunessy. My cousins. Freddy grabbed Shaunessy around the neck and knuckled his head. *I'm still taller than you, bro!* he said.

No you not! Shaunessy laughed, trying to knuckle Freddy's head back.

Hey, Gwen said to me, and smiled. It was a real smile.

Gwen was about my height. She was wearing a white halter dress that went all the way down to her ankles. Beneath it, I could see the tips of white platform sandals. She wasn't wearing any makeup and her cornrows were pulled together with a piece of yarn. I stared at her, trying not to stare at her. She didn't look like she played basketball, but she didn't look like she spent all her time trying to make herself look cute either.

Hey, I said back. *Nice meeting you.*

You sound like Freddy, Gwen said. *I like your New York accent.*

I like yours, I said.

This is just New Orleans, she said. *Everybody talks like this where we come from.*

There was a soft edge in the way she talked. *New Orleans* rolling into one long word with the *e*'s growing silent: *N'Orlins.* I had heard that edge in the voices of some of the people on the block. The ones who had come to Brooklyn from places like South Carolina, Texas, and, like Freddy's people, Louisiana. I liked it. Already I liked everything about Gwen. The dusty hem of her too-long dress, the fraying yarn on her cornrows. The way she looked at my wrinkled Knicks shirt and dirty basketball shoes without frowning.

This is Sage, everybody, Freddy announced.

She your girlfriend? Shaunessy asked. He raised his eyebrows up and down quickly and laughed. *You lucky. She's pretty.*

I could feel my ears get hot.

Friend, Freddy said. He grabbed Shaunessy again, but this

time, he just hugged him. *Not every girl is somebody's girl-friend, fool. Sage can run you over on the court.*

Shaunessy looked at me but didn't say anything.

Then Freddy's mother was at the door, out of breath and twisting her hair back into the bun it was falling out of.

Freddy, help them with those suitcases. There must have been six or seven huge suitcases sitting on the sidewalk. I hadn't even noticed the driver pulling them out of the trunk and driving away, but there were the suitcases, and the cab was gone.

I can help too . . . I started to say.

We'll take care of all this, Freddy's mother said as I climbed off the stoop to get out of the way of it all. *Freddy'll see you later, love.*

Can't she stay and hang out with us, Ma?

Freddy's mom winked at me. *Come on by later, Sage,* she said. *After we get these Louisiana people settled and dusted off.*

I put the last cookie in my pocket and started heading down Palmetto Street.

Don't forget to tell your mama her Avon order should be coming in next week, Freddy's mom called to me. *And I have the new catalog if she wants to take a look.*

I turned back toward them and nodded. Shaunessy was carrying a heavy-looking suitcase up the stoop and eyeing my basketball. *Can you dunk?* he asked.

Not yet. I have to grow another couple of feet first.

He smiled, looking relieved. Then, like the rest of them, he disappeared into Freddy's building.

23

FREDDY CALLED ME THE NEXT morning to see if me and my mom wanted to come over that night for some New Orleans cooking.

I could hear people talking at Freddy's house, their voices coming through the phone. I could hear a man laughing—hard and loud like what he'd just heard was the funniest thing in the world.

The only New Orleans food I ever had were little donuts called beignets that Freddy's mom had made us once. They were fried and covered with powdered sugar and the best thing I'd ever eaten in my life.

She making beignets? I asked.

Yup.

Bet!

24

FREDDY'S APARTMENT WAS FILLED WITH people when my mother and I got there. The O'Jays album was on the record player and the song "Family Reunion" filled the whole apartment.

Y'all finally made it, Freddy's mother said, coming out of the kitchen with a plate filled with food. *Make sure you get yourselves something to eat—I made gumbo, rice, etouffee—you name it, it's in that kitchen.*

I walked over to Shaunessy, Freddy, and Gwen just as they started dancing. *You gotta dance to this one, Sage,* Shaunessy said.

I shook my head.

I can show you how. Gwen looked at me. *It's not hard.*

I seen her dance before, Freddy said. *She's just being shy.*

Look at this move, Shaunessy said. He did a spin and slid down into a split. *Can you do that, Sage?*

Does she even want to? Freddy said. *Nobody trying to do your fake James Brown moves.*

Shaunessy got up again. *You know how to do the Funky Chicken?*

Of course she does. How you gonna live in Brooklyn and not know that.

Someone changed the record to Earth, Wind & Fire, and I joined in the dancing. I had been dancing since forever. The Funky Chicken was easy, but when Shaunessy tried to do it, he looked like he'd fall over. I looked at Gwen. She was wearing a different long dress. This one was dark blue and made out of some kind of shiny material. The sandals were gone now, and she was dancing barefoot with her eyes closed. She looked like she was far away from everything and everybody. She and Shaunessy made me wish I had cousins. I'd probably be less quiet if I had some. And our house would be like Freddy's house was now—filled with music and talking and dancing.

I heard my mother laugh and looked over to see her with

a plate of food, talking with Freddy's mother. Maybe she wanted cousins too.

What's et-two-fay? I said over the music.

Shaunessy's eyes got wide. *You never ate etouffee?! Girl, let me go make you a plate!*

In the kitchen, Shaunessy grabbed a bowl from a stack and started scooping rice from a big pot on the stove. Then he opened another pot and scooped a soup with shrimp, peppers, onions, and other stuff over the rice.

This, he said, getting a spoon from the bunch of them beside the bowls and handing it to me, *is coming to you straight from God's house by way of New Orleans.*

That's what our mama says, Gwen said. *My brother acting like those his own words. Taste it, though.*

Shaunessy gave a little bow and handed me the bowl. He and Freddy and Gwen waited for me to taste it.

I don't really like shrimp . . . I said.

Shaunessy slapped his head and looked at Freddy. *You. Have.*

A. Friend. Who. Doesn't. Like. Shrimp?! How is that even possible? That's like not liking air!

Just taste it, Sage, Gwen said. *I like a lot of stuff now that I never did before. Including shrimp!*

I thought for a minute of all the things I didn't like—dresses, dolls, sandals. Shrimp.

But I closed my eyes, like Gwen did when she danced, and I tasted the etouffee. It was spicy and warm, and I took another spoonful.

I knew it! Shaunessy said. *You like it, right?*

I took another, bigger spoonful. And then another. I couldn't eat it fast enough. It felt like it melted inside my mouth. My bowl was empty in no time.

Not sure, I said. *I mean . . . maybe I need a little more to make sure.*

Gwen laughed and filled my bowl up again. *See? Don't be sure you'll hate things. I used to be like that.*

Not me, Shaunessy said. *I like everything!*

Then Gwen made bowls for Shaunessy, Freddy, and herself. We carried them back into the living room, squeezed past a whole lot of dancing grown-ups, and sat by the window.

In the distance, I could hear the sound of sirens. But the laughter and the music and the deliciousness of the etouffee was louder.

25

I WENT TO SAY GOODBYE to Freddy's cousins when they were ready to head home to New Orleans.

You gonna write to me, Sage? Gwen asked. She had written her address on a piece of notebook paper, her name and a small heart beneath it. I nodded, taking the paper and hugging her first, then Shaunessy.

We coming back next summer, Shaunessy said. *And the one after that and the one after that and . . . Just saying, no need for every-body to get all blubbery.* But he wiped his eyes with the back of his hand before climbing into the taxi beside his sister.

When everybody was inside and the taxicab had pulled away, Freddy and I stood on his stoop, still waving.

Want to go shoot hoops? I asked.

Freddy looked in the direction of the now-faded taxi, his eyes dark and sad. *Nah.*

For real? No hoops?

I think I'm just gonna go upstairs and lie down for a while, he said. *Kinda tired. Sorry, Sage.*

But it's only four o'clock.

I miss my cousins, he said.

Then, without saying anything else, he disappeared into his building.

26

FOR SO MANY YEARS, WHENEVER I left my house, I walked by the red fire alarm on the corner of our block. When I was very young, I used to hug it. As I got older, I ran my fingers over the word LIFT. Sometimes I wrapped my hand around the handle.

This is all it takes, I thought. Lift the handle and run.

A bell would ring in the firehouse on Knickerbocker Avenue. And soon we'd hear the sirens. Still, there'd be enough time to run and hide. Enough time to get away. I didn't wonder why kids did this. I was a kid and I knew the joy of running away laughing. I knew the glory of finding ways to confuse adults. I knew there was *something* . . . maybe the word is *powerful*. One pull of the handle and I could move a whole firehouse full of trucks to my block.

Lifting that handle wouldn't bring my father back. And still . . .

LIFT ME, the handle begged. *Lift me.*

27

THAT SUMMER, WHEN IT WAS too hot to play ball in the middle of the day, Freddy and I sat in my living room going through *Sport* magazine and trading basketball cards. My mother had put a box fan in one of the windows, and it blew hot air on us as we leaned over the stats of Walt Frazier, Dave DeBusschere, and Bill Bradley.

When the sun was finally low enough for a game, Freddy and I ran to the park, where the sound of sirens disappeared beneath our shouting of *Shoot!* and *Pass it!* and *Bruh, how did you even miss that easy shot?*

As the basketball rolled off my fingers and into the hoop, I talked about my dreams of going pro. *Point guard,* I said, dribbling long and laying the ball up. *First woman in the NBA. The world's not ready for the next #33.*

So you trying to be wearing Kareem's number now? Randy said. *Never gonna happen. Maybe one day there'll be a ladies' basketball team or something, but nobody's gonna let you roll with the dudes no matter how good you are.*

Knicks gonna let me roll, I said, ignoring him. *Not waiting for some ladies' team.*

Sage wants to be rich and famous like the pros, Freddy said.

Nah. I dribbled the ball through all of them and hooked it into the basket. *I don't care about being rich. I just want to play the game.*

28

ONE SUNDAY NIGHT, AS I sat down on the floor to watch *The Wonderful World of Disney*, a public service ad came on.

It started with a huge fire, its flames taking up the whole television screen. Then the camera pulled back to show us that the fire lived inside the eyes of a bear named Smokey and he was always watching it.

Only you, Smokey said as he looked at me, *can prevent forest fires.*

Then the camera closed in on his face. And we could see that Smokey the Bear was crying.

29

BEFORE IT WAS A NEIGHBORHOOD with wood-framed houses, bodegas, basketball courts, and double-dutch ropes spinning on every street, my neighborhood was a forest filled with trees. Before it was Bushwick, it was the land of the Lenape, who lived among the trees and didn't need a bear coming on the TV screen on a Sunday night to remind them about the dangers of fire. They understood smoke and flame and the power of the woods.

When the Dutch explorers came, they called this place Boswijck, "little town in the woods." But then they cut the trees down to make room for houses. So the woods became the wood that became the wooden houses.

Bluestone was laid over earthen ground to make sidewalks. Stoops leading to the upper floors were slabbed. Windows and doorways were framed. Tar roofs were laid so that from above, it must have looked like a long black street.

The blocks that grew out of the woods were named for the trees that once thrived there—Linden, Cypress, Woodbine, Evergreen, Cornelia, Palmetto.

We lived in the shadow of the forest. The long-ago history of it mostly forgotten.

Most of the blocks were treeless now.

So we lived in the *once was* of the Lenape and the trees.

And our homes were burning.

Who would remember this place?

Who would remember *us*?

30

SOMETIMES FREDDY'S EYES GOT SUCH a sadness around the edges that they looked like they'd gone back to someplace before. They became different eyes. Still blue-gray but . . . *different*. The first time it happened, we were walking up his block on our way to the park, and he just stopped and looked back in the direction we'd just come from.

Hey, I said. *You forget something?*

But Freddy didn't answer me.

You okay?

Yeah, he finally said. *I guess. I think I'm missing where we moved from. I don't know. Something we just passed gave me a feeling. That ever happen to you?*

I don't . . . think so.

It's like a ghost, Freddy said. *Something back there. Like right back there when we passed those two ladies laughing. Something just gave me a feeling like this all happened before . . .*

Freddy stood there a few minutes more, then started walking again.

Weird, he said.

For real. Then I thought of a question. *Why'd you move here, anyway?*

Freddy put his hands in his pockets. He looked over his shoulder one more time, then started walking faster. *We moved here from the Bronx. I told you before.*

But you never told me why you moved.

We were standing on the corner of Knickerbocker now, just outside the park. Freddy leaned against a graffiti-covered brick wall. Right above him, somebody had painted a red heart. The sun shifted, landing on Freddy and the heart.

Too many fires there too, Freddy said.

Your house burn? The one in the Bronx? A part of me didn't want to know, but I asked anyway.

Freddy shook his head. *Nah. Not while we lived there. It's gone now, though.*

He looked at me. *My dad didn't know about Palmetto Street when he found our apartment. He thought it was gonna be better in Brooklyn.*

I leaned next to him on the wall. We both squinted against the sun.

What did we look like to the people passing by us? What would we look like if someone had taken a picture of us? Freddy with his wild hair and beautiful eyes. Me with a frizzing braid and a too-big Knicks T-shirt that had once been my dad's hanging down over my shorts.

And if we're all on our way to being a part of the *once was,* were Freddy and I already fading?

I guess this place is better in some ways, Freddy said. *It's safe to walk around. And people just let you play basketball without making you feel bad if you miss a shot or something.*

I moved closer until our shoulders were touching.

I'm glad your dad didn't know the other stuff, I said.

And Freddy nodded. *Yeah. Me too.*

31

THAT YEAR, THE STRANGEST THINGS hollowed my throat and brought the sting of tears to my eyes. The way Freddy's frayed jeans puddled over his ragged sneakers. The sun and the graffiti heart and me and Freddy against that wall.

The fires and the tear in Smokey's eye. The *Daily News* calling our neighborhood The Matchbox.

The way some boys laughed when I said I was going to play pro ball.

And other things too. Like my mother sitting at the kitchen table staring at her wedding photo.

Again and again, I found myself blinking back a sadness I didn't understand.

Maybe I had a ghost too. Only it wasn't somewhere behind me, like Freddy's. My ghost was inside of me. Here now and then gone again.

32

TOWARD THE END OF JULY, heavy rains emptied the streets. The burnt-out buildings darkened to near black, and the charred mattresses sagged even more with the weight of the water.

In the park, water pooled on the empty basketball courts and dripped from the orange rims. Still, even as it poured, I stood at the foul line shooting free throws by myself.

As I moved farther back to work on my outside shot, a teen-age boy appeared. He was tall and wide-shouldered and stood watching me.

One-on-one? I asked.

No, he said.

I glanced at him, then shrugged and went back to shooting. I'd never seen him around before. Maybe he didn't know I could play. I shot from outside and watched the ball sink easily into the basket. Thunder rumbled and the sky got darker. I dribbled the ball between my legs, took another shot, and sunk it again. I could feel the boy's eyes on me.

Then he was speaking. For a minute, inside the sounds of thunder and falling rain, his words blurred. But slowly they made their way to me.

What kind of girl are you, anyway?

What're you talking about?

You shoot that ball like you think you a dude or something.

Suddenly I was scared. There wasn't anyone else around. If Freddy and the others had been there, they'd have had my back. But they weren't.

The boy took a step closer. I grabbed my ball and held it to my chest. I wanted it to be a shield against his words and the way he was looking at me. *What kind of girl are you?*

He smiled then, but it wasn't a kind smile. I held tighter to my ball, waiting. I didn't know what I was waiting for.

I should punch you in the face just to show you you ain't a dude, that's what I should do!

I stood there trying to figure out what to do. If I ran, would he be able to catch me?

Look at you, the boy said. *Looking all scared. I'm gonna make believe you're a real girl and walk away. This time.*

He took another step closer, so close I could feel the heat of his breath against my face. He grabbed the ball out of my hands and threw it across the park. I closed my eyes hard and heard the soft, faraway bounce of it.

When I finally opened my eyes again, he had turned and was heading away from me. I folded my arms tight across my chest and watched him run through the park. He grabbed my ball from a puddle and kept on running.

Then he was gone. And my ball was gone. Maybe I was gone too.

I opened my mouth, trying to take in deep gulps of rainy air, but still, I couldn't breathe. When the tears came, they came hard. The sky lit up, followed by another crash of thunder. But my crying felt louder.

Rain dripped from every part of me, sticking my shirt to my back, my shorts to my legs. But I couldn't move. Couldn't run home. Something held me inside that empty park with my ball gone and the rain and thunder coming hard. I felt alone, and wrong inside my big hands and long legs and skinny arms. My braid, dripping with rain, felt wrong. The soaking-wet basketball shorts and tube socks and drenched sneakers—none of it felt right anymore.

I'm me! I screamed. *I'm Sage! That's what kind of girl I am!*

The back of my throat burned from the screaming, but nothing echoed back at me.

I'm Sage, I said again. But this time the words came in a whisper. So soft. So almost *disappeared.*

After a long time, I wiped my face with my hand and took a deep, slow breath. My sneakers squished as I headed out of the park.

Basketball had always run like blood through my veins. I had always been so deep inside the heat of the game, the burn of it. And I had always been the flame.

I looked at my empty hands. I had other basketballs, but this one had been my father's. A Rawlings he'd had in college. It was old and smooth and had been held by him. And then by me. For years and years.

What kind of girl are you?

For a long time, I had thought there was only one thing that could take all that you loved away.

And that one thing was fire.

33

THAT AFTERNOON, ALONE IN MY bedroom, I peeled off my soaking-wet clothes and hung my dad's Knicks shirt over my chair to dry. I put the basketball shorts and the socks in my trash can and pushed my wet high-tops to the back of my closet. I stood in the center of my room in pajama bottoms and a plain white T-shirt and looked around. An old poster of Julius Erving stared down at me. Maybe he was asking the same question the boy in the park had asked, so I pulled his picture from my wall.

I kept seeing the boy's face, the hatred beneath the confusion. I saw him fake a lunge at me. Saw him grab my ball and throw it. Saw him grab my ball again and keep on running. And his words and my ball became the same thing. I saw my ball again, but his words were written all over it now. *What kind of girl are you, anyway?*

I didn't know it then, but already I was forgetting the stats of every basketball player I'd ever loved. I was putting away my crossover. And my layup. And my post-up and behind-the-back dribble and down-low dribble and sneak attack. I was forgetting my outside shot, my three-pointer.

I was burying my dream of one day growing to be six feet tall and smashing the ball into the basket.

I was . . . disappearing.

34

WHERE'S YOUR BALL? FREDDY ASKED a few days later.
The rain had finally stopped and the sky was bright blue and
cloudless.

Forgot it, I said as we headed to the park.

You never forget your ball. He looked at me.

I don't have it! Okay?

Hey. Hey. What's up, Sage? You mad at me?

I wanted to tell him everything. I wanted to run home and
hide in my room.

Nah, I said. *Just gonna watch today.*

*All the time I've known you, you never said you didn't want to
play ball.*

Freddy looked at me again and waited. When I didn't say anything, he shrugged, and at the park he pulled Randy and some other guys together for a game.

I leaned against the chain-link fence, watching them miss easy shots, get the ball stolen, foul each other, and throw wild passes.

After a while, I told them I was heading home.

You sure you okay, Sage? Freddy said. *Want me to come hang with you a bit?*

I shook my head. *Just gonna read or something,* I said, already heading out of the park. I gave them a backwards wave and kept walking.

And for a long time, I tried to forget about basketball. Forget how playing ball made me feel like the little kids on the mattresses.

Like I was flying.

Like I was fierce.

Like I was free.

35

MY MOTHER WORKED IN THE main office of a high school in Manhattan. Since she was off during the summer too, we usually took a vacation in August—Disneyland once, Peg Leg Bates' Country Club upstate *a lot*.

Peg Leg Bates' place was my favorite. The owner had a wooden leg and used to be a dancer. He opened the country club for Black people because no other clubs would let us in. I'd never seen so many rich-looking Black people in one place, swimming and playing tennis and sitting out on the grounds having picnics. I spent most of my time there on the basketball court.

But that summer, we stayed home because my mother was saving money for the new house she kept talking about. *And* she had decided to write a book. So she spent long hours at her typewriter in a small room downstairs she had turned into an office.

Every day I wanted to run down the stairs and tell my mother about the boy in the park. But for some reason I couldn't. My mother was beautiful. Her nails were polished. Her hair was neat. How would she ever understand what it meant to feel like you were walking crooked in the world. Like some part of you wasn't . . . wasn't right.

I had taken one of my other basketballs out of the closet. It needed air and felt too new and slippery. At night I lay on my back, tossing it up into the air, trying to feel *something*. But nothing came back. Whatever had been there felt like ashes. For a long time.

But toward the end of summer, I took a deep breath and headed down to my mother's office.

The rain had returned, bringing clouds so dark, it looked like it was almost night in the middle of the afternoon.

What're you doing? I asked. My mother jumped at the sound of my voice and opened her eyes.

Why do you sneak up on people like some kind of ghost, Sage?

If you had been writing instead of sleeping—

I was just resting my eyes.

You were snoring, Ma.

She grabbed a pencil from her desk and gently threw it at me. I dodged it easily.

Was not! I was thinking, she said. But she was smiling, so I walked in and started to lower myself down on the pullout couch across from her chair.

No sitting, Sage. You'll start talking and I'll stop writing.

I ignored her and sat anyway.

Do you think I'm pretty? I pulled some of the hair frizzing by my ears around my finger, twirling it.

I think you're beautiful, my mother said. She put a new sheet of paper in her typewriter, centered it, and put her fingers on the keys. She could type without looking at the letters. When she did, it looked like magic.

You're saying that because you're my mom. But really, do you think I'm pretty? I turned my face in profile and lifted my chin. *Like when I do this—do you think I'm pretty . . . pretty like a girl should be pretty?*

I held my head very still, waiting, my eyes sliding toward her.

My mother turned to me. She looked at me like she had a hundred questions she didn't know how to ask. *What do you mean, like a girl should be pretty?*

I didn't say anything. Just kept holding my head sideways and still.

Did someone say something?

No, I lied. *I'm just asking.*

Is there someone you're interested in attract—

Ew! Ma! No! I'm twelve!

She stared at me. My neck was starting to hurt, so I turned my head toward her. *I just wanted to know what you thought,* I said softly. *Not as a mom, though. As somebody telling the truth.*

Yes, Sage, she said. *Inside and out. You're beautiful and pretty and kind. And if anyone ever says something different, they're just . . . stupid.*

Ma! You always tell me not to say stupid!

They're not bright, then. How about that? She searched my face. *Sage? What's going on?*

I'm not kind, I said.

You always make time for those ragged little kids in the neighborhood. I've seen it.

They can't help being ragged.

Exactly. See? Kind. And beautiful.

The rain started coming down harder as I headed back upstairs and climbed onto the cushioned bench by the living room window.

For a long time, I sat with my arms wrapped around my legs, staring out at the storm. I had never *not* been able to tell my mother everything. But now I couldn't. It was like that boy had *changed* something. And that change had left me in this new place.

A new place where I felt completely, one hundred percent alone.

36

IN THE BATHROOM MIRROR, I stared at my face, pulling my lips to one side, then the other. I leaned in closer to the mirror and smiled until the dimple at the top of my cheek deepened. Were my eyelashes too thick and curly? I tried to flatten them between my thumb and forefinger, but when I let go, they curled right back up again. My braid stopped just between my shoulder blades and always came loose at the bottom like a piece of unraveling rope. I unbraided it and it hung in three crimped sections. I tried shaking them, but that didn't change anything.

What kind of girl are you, anyway?

I stuck my tongue out at my reflection, quickly pulled my hair back into a braid, and went into the kitchen. I tried to remember the day my father gave me his basketball, but it felt like it had always been *ours*. A siren wailed in the distance.

There was a box of matches on the counter beside the stove

that we used when the igniter didn't catch. I looked at them for a long time before grabbing them and heading back to the bathroom, this time locking the door behind me. For a while I just sat on the side of the bathtub, striking them and watching their flame burn bright orange, then blue, before I dropped the match into the toilet.

Then something shook inside of me. I don't know how to explain it. I felt angry and hollow and miserable all at the same time. I struck another match and held it to the roll of toilet paper attached to the bathroom door. The toilet paper went up in flames so quickly, I jumped back and heard myself screaming as the curtain above the roll caught fire and black smoke quickly filled the tiny bathroom. Maybe a minute passed before I realized I was trapped on the other side of the fire. I couldn't breathe suddenly. Black smoke had replaced the air. I tried to cough and couldn't. No breath was coming in or going out of me.

Where did the time go?

I saw my mother appear from the other side of the burning door, a pail of water in her hands. Maybe she was screaming too. I only remember what I saw, not what I heard.

Smoke filled my nostrils. My eyes. My mouth.

Then I was stumbling out, gulping air like water. Each breath a little less painful than the one before. Maybe my mother was asking *Why?* I don't know. I don't remember.

Long after the fire was out, though, my mother kept dousing the bathroom door. Later, she would tell me *You don't always know when it's completely out. Sometimes the tiniest flame can hide inside a wall. Waiting.*

She asked *What were you thinking?*

She said *Don't even ask to leave this house for the next month! No more basketball! Nothing, Sage. Nothing!*

I said *I'm sorry.*

I didn't say *There's no more basketball anyway.*

I didn't ask *Where would I even go?*

37

THE FIRE THAT KILLED MY father had been caused by frayed wires hidden in the walls of a building in downtown Brooklyn. The walls were smoking when the firefighters arrived. More wires caught until finally the fire burst from the ceiling, raining down beams and sparks and flames.

They told my mother it happened so quickly, my father didn't suffer. Didn't know what hit him. They told my mother he died a hero.

But I know they were wrong now. At the first sight of the first flame, you are already suffering. Already searching for your breath even if it's just to scream.

At the first hiss of fiery air, you know the world as you've always known it is about to be changed forever.

38

MY MOTHER HID THE MATCHES after the bathroom fire.

As I moved through our house, she watched me.

Her eyes said *Who are you?*

Her eyes asked again and again *What happened to my Sage?*

39

IT COULD'VE BEEN WORSE. I could've still have *wanted* to go outside. And I could've been grounded in a tiny apartment, bumping eyes and shoulders with my mother at every turn. But the courts felt like part of the *once was* now, and we had a big apartment—four rooms from back to front upstairs and three rooms downstairs, with a long hallway lined with wood paneling.

And I had two spots to watch the rest of summer pass me by.

Each morning I made my way to our kitchen, where I sat for hours watching the world outside in our backyard. Cats of all colors roamed freely through it. In the house behind ours, four small children found uses for an old car tire. I watched them jump into it and out again, roll it around their backyard, turn it on its side and attempt to fill it with a garden hose. And when that failed, they sprayed each other with water, their laughter echoing across and up to me.

In the afternoon, I sat on the bench in the living room window, watching the street. Most days the sun was bright and I pressed my forehead against the warm glass to see as much as I could of the block.

One day I saw my old friend Angie and some other girls playing handball against the factory wall on the corner. I watched them, remembering the days when we were all still friends and how mad they'd get when I'd quit in the middle of a game of double dutch or hopscotch to go shoot hoops with the boys in the park. I hated that I had to make a choice—basketball with the boys or playing with the girls.

I don't know when it happened, when we stopped being like those little kids on the mattresses who always played together, not caring if you were a boy or a girl. But something changed around the time we turned ten. We started separating. Maybe we had learned it at school, with the teachers always lining boys up on one side and girls on the other. And then those lines moved outside the school and onto the playground and then onto our block, until the day came when I saw some boys I knew heading to the park, turned to the girls I'd been playing jacks with, and said *I'll be back later.* But as I got up from where I was sitting with them on the curb, Angie shook her head and looked up at me. *You don't have to come back, Sage,* she said. *We're good. Go play with your* boys.

Maybe I never came back. Or maybe they never let me.

40

ANGIE AND THE GIRLS FELT far away. Everything they did seemed unfamiliar to me—the way they leaned into each other to whisper, the raised eyebrows of the girls being whispered to, the delighted giggles that followed the whispering. Maybe that's what that boy meant when he said *What kind of girl are you, anyway?* For a long time, I only knew one other kind of girl besides myself. The kind like Angie and her friends who painted their nails, curled their hair, moved in tight circles, and whispered secrets to each other. The kind that looked at me the way that boy did. As though they were asking the same question.

I thought about Freddy's cousin Gwen. She didn't love basketball or wear a Knicks shirt every day, but still, she was *different*. So there were two of us.

Somewhere out in the world, maybe there were more.

41

SOME DAYS I SAT AT the front window watching the little kids race. As a line of them ran down the street, disappeared out of my view beyond the oak tree at the end of the block, and reappeared minutes later arguing about who had won, I remembered myself at that age. I had once been the fastest kid on the block. No one else ran the way I did—taking off my sneakers and socks, then tearing down the middle of the street barefoot. Once, running felt like flying to me—my feet lifting off the hot tar of the street and landing almost soundlessly, only to lift again just as they touched down. My hands open wide, slicing the air. My head down. The air in my lungs always on the edge of being completely gone, but still, I kept on running.

42

SO MANY MORNINGS AFTER THE fire, Freddy rang my bell. But my mother only let me crack the door wide enough to tell him I still couldn't come outside.

You ever *getting off of punishment?* he asked. And, wide-eyed, he whispered *What the heck did you do, anyway?*

I couldn't tell Freddy the truth, so I just stood there peeking out the door, watching disappointment show up in the way he pulled his lips to the side of his face and looked off toward the park.

I messed up, I said. *Don't know when my mom's letting me out of this house again.*

Another time he came, he said *That chump Dooey from Putnam Ave beat me and Randy by two points the other day. Park ain't the same without you, Sage. I figured by now you'd be off your basketball strike and ready to play with us again.*

I didn't say anything.

What did you do? he asked again.

But still, I couldn't tell him. The fire was somewhere inside of me—a shame so searing, I knew I'd never forget it.

43

LATE ONE NIGHT, WHEN I got up to go to the bathroom, I looked out the window just to see if anyone was out there. For a minute the street was empty, the streetlight flickering bright orange, the chalk drawings and hopscotch games gleaming beneath it. I saw a stray kitten dart under a parked car, then run inside my neighbor's gate and through the metal bars of their open window. The box fan in the living room window whirred softly, but that was the only sound. No sirens wailing. No car horns.

Mr. Jolly from down the block appeared out of the darkness. He was carrying a small bucket, and his white T-shirt was bright against the night. We called him Mr. Jolly because he was always whistling. But now Mr. Jolly was dead quiet as he headed to the corner. There, under the streetlight, I saw him pull a small paintbrush from the bucket and paint the handle of the fire alarm. His hand moved slowly up and down.

The bathroom called to me. Then sleep. Then dreams of Mr. Jolly's hand with the paintbrush moving slowly up and down, up and down. And me waking to wonder if it had all been a dream.

44

SEEING MR. JOLLY AT THE fire alarm had not been a dream. And it wasn't paint. He had used ink on the alarm. Black ink that, in the humidity of summer, wouldn't dry.

I only found this out days later when I stood at the window watching him chase two boys across the street. When he caught the taller one, he made him hold out his blackened palms. The boy stood there wide-eyed and shaking.

I'm so sorry, Mr. Jolly. For real, I'm so sorry.

Show me where you live, Mr. Jolly said. *I want to talk to your mama. Does she know you out here getting real people killed with those false alarms?*

I'm so sorry, the boy kept saying, and I felt sorry for him. I thought about the many times I'd walked by that fire alarm, itching to pull it. Thought about the fire I'd set in our own bathroom.

In the distance, I could hear the fire trucks growing closer.

I closed the window then. Maybe Mr. Jolly was our own Smokey the Bear. Maybe for a while our block was safe.

45

THE WORLD I KNEW WAS Linden and Putnam and Gates and Woodbine and Palmetto Street. The world was everyone I knew and everything I saw. And back then I thought this would always be so. But that summer, I learned the world had other plans.

My mother and I were the only people on our block who didn't attend church, and our neighbor Mrs. Peat often stopped us on the street to invite us to go with her. But my mom said no, that church wasn't for her. *Then let me take Sage sometime,* Mrs. Peat said. And that's how it started that one Sunday a month, my mother made me put on the one dress I owned and tag along behind Mrs. Peat to Holy Mount Baptist Church.

Usually, I found ways to zone out when the reverend was speaking. I counted hats or looked for the shiniest shoes or the most beat-up ones. I looked through the Bible to find rhyming words or searched for the nicest earrings or biggest afros among the singers in the choir. Sometimes, if the sun was shining outside, I just stared at the light coming though the stained glass.

One Sunday, I was staring at the back of a little kid's head three rows in front of me. He had a heart-shaped patch of white hair just behind his left ear. When he turned, I saw that it was Jacob. He waved at me, and I remembered how he had held my hand all the way to the candy store that day Freddy found the wallet. How could I not have noticed the patch of white before?

As we left church that day, Jacob ran up to me. *Hey, candy girl,* he said. His suit was about two sizes too big, but someone had hemmed the sleeves and the legs of his pants.

I got these, he said, pulling a hand filled with plastic-wrapped peppermints from his pocket.

One for you, he said, handing me two of them. *And can you give one to Freddy? He bought me candy, remember?*

I nodded, smiling down at him.

God gave me His heart, he said.

Huh?

I saw you looking at my head. He pointed to the white patch. *That's what my mama says. I was born like this cuz God gave me His heart.*

Jacob! He turned toward his mother. Her headscarf and flip-flops were gone now, and she was wearing a blue dress and matching hat.

Coming, Mama! he said, then turned back to me. *You have a blessed day. And don't forget to give Freddy the candy!*

Then he ran off.

And that was the last time I saw him. Running after his mother, that white heart of God fading down Wilson Avenue.

Three days later, Jacob died in a fire.

46

MRS. PEAT CAME TO LET us know the plans for Jacob's funeral, and when my mother asked if I wanted to go, I nodded.

You don't have to, my mother said after she'd closed the door. *There're other ways to say goodbye, Sage.*

I should go, I said. *I like Jacob.* Then I caught myself and started to say *liked*, but that felt wrong. Jacob didn't feel past tense to me. He wasn't a part of the *once was*. He was still Jacob. The boy who did flips on mattresses, loved candy, and had God's heart on his head.

So I went to Jacob's funeral and sat between Mrs. Peat and my mother. Everyone in the neighborhood seemed to be there. Freddy in a dark suit sitting between his mom and dad. Angie with her little sister and her mother. The kids who played with Jacob on the mattresses looking frightened in their shirts and tiny ties. The old men from the block who sat in folding chairs at the corner. The old ladies who hung out of their windows watching everything happening on the block. Teenagers in couples and alone. So many people that the deacons had to leave the church doors open for the people who couldn't fit inside.

As the choir climbed onto the stage in their gold-and-purple robes and began singing "Joy Comes in the Morning," I thought about Jacob. I thought about his torn T-shirt and green shorts that day he did flips on Palmetto Street. I thought about him in his too-big suit, the half adult tooth that was still growing in. I thought about him putting those two pieces of candy in my hand, me eating both of them later, one right after the other, and forgetting to tell Freddy about it.

The choir's voices rose up. I could see Freddy's back from where I was sitting, his shoulders shaking. I lowered my head to hide my tears, wondering why they were singing about joy. My mother put her arm around me, and I blinked hard. Then the preacher was saying what a good boy Jacob had been. How well he did in first grade and how on Sundays he always tithed, giving half of his allowance to the Lord.

All around me, people were nodding, waving their hands in the air, and saying *Amen* and *Yes, Lord*. I wanted to say something too, but my own words were jammed inside my throat. Every time I swallowed, the words felt like they'd spill out in tears.

For a long time after my father died, the fires felt far away. Even when my own bathroom was filled with smoke and flame, some part of me had a sense that I'd be all right. And maybe this is what I thought about everyone I knew. That even with the fires, we'd all be all right. Maybe I thought fire had already taken everything from us that it could. But it didn't feel that way now.

God is good, the preacher was saying. And the congregation echoed back *Every day.* The women's wide-brimmed hats fluttered with the nodding.

But Jacob had died.

Joy comes in the *mourning*? Is that what the preacher was saying? I wanted to raise my hand and ask. But I knew it would rise shakily into the air, so I folded my hands on my lap, let the music rising from the organ move through my body, up my neck, across my shoulders . . . I thought about that white patch behind Jacob's ear. God's heart.

Weeping may tarry for the night, the preacher was saying. *But joy comes with the morning.*

Mourning. Morning.

The fire had broken out early in the morning. Had Jacob been sound asleep? Did he wake to the smell of smoke moving across his room? Did he cough? Call out for his mama? And where was his mother? I lifted my head and looked around the church. Then I saw her—in the front row, dressed all in black. Her head bent. Her shoulders rising and falling. Rising and falling.

There was a stained-glass Black Jesus behind the preacher's head, His hands open, welcoming all of us. But on the right side of the church, there was plywood where another stained-glass window had once been. The wall below burned a dark brown.

How much more are we going to lose? I wanted to ask the preacher.

I brought my hands to my face and closed my eyes. I prayed for the church. I prayed for Jacob and every kid in Bushwick waking to the smell of smoke. I prayed for all the hearts on all the heads everywhere. Amen.

My mother put her hand on my back, moved it in slow circles. This, too, felt like prayer.

47

MAYBE IT WAS BECAUSE OF Jacob that my mother set me free again.

Life is short, she said softly after the funeral. *God bless the child.*

No further than the end of the block, she said. *And no, you can't go over to anybody's house, so don't even ask. God forbid you try to burn someone else's . . .* she started to say, then stopped herself, pulled me to her, and hugged me. *We're going to be all right, Sage.*

I know.

She kissed my forehead and said *Go get some fresh air.*

I raced down the stairs before she could change her mind.

48

THE OUTSIDE WORLD FELT LOUD and bright. Two little boys took turns rolling each other on a skateboard, and the twin girls who lived down the block stumbled past me on matching silver skates.

Hi, Sage, they said at the same time.

I knew their names but couldn't tell them apart, so I just said *Hey, twins* and watched them holding on to the gates as they rolled and stumbled down the block.

After a while, Angie, her little sister, and some others came around the corner. Two of the girls with her were sisters who lived on Cornelia Street. The one who I knew, Samara, was the same age as me and Angie.

Hey, she said.

Hey, yourself, I said back.

How come you're not at the park?

I shrugged. *Didn't feel like it.*

But you always feel like playing basketball.

I shrugged again.

Well, we got a rope, Samara said. *If you want in.*

I'll watch for now, I said.

Suit yourself, Angie's little sister said. She started untangling the rope, but Angie came onto the stoop and sat down beside me.

It's too hot to jump anyway, Angie said. She leaned her head against my leg. It felt good there. Familiar. Like old times.

Feel like I haven't seen you in forever, Sage.

I was on punishment.

For what?

Stupid stuff.

Parents always be doing that, Angie said. *I can't stand them sometimes.*

Yeah, I said.

Somebody put a whole bunch of flowers in that lot on Palmetto where Jacob was always playing, Angie said. *They put one of his school pictures too.*

I don't know if I can go look at that. Too sad.

Yeah, Angie said. *He was a cute kid.*

You ever seen him do those flips? I asked. *On the mattress?*

Angie lifted her head to look at me. *I saw him do, like, this triple twirl in the air once. He just kept spinning and spinning.*

I saw him do that, I said. *He was magic.*

She put her head back on my knee.

Yeah, she said. *I like to think he's still out there flying.*

49

AFTER ANGIE LEFT, SOME KIDS ran by, saying that a dog had been hit by a car on the corner of Knickerbocker and Madison.

The guy didn't even stop, one of them said. *He just kept driving, man, like that dog was nothing! Like the dog was just a can that had rolled into the street.*

I should have stayed where I was. But like a bunch of other kids, I bolted from my stoop and ran to the corner.

The dog was black and tan with a black circle over his left eye. His mouth was open, and the teeth inside were white and sharp. A little boy I didn't know squatted beside him, trying to get him to open his eyes again.

I bent down beside the boy and whispered *He's in heaven now.*

No he's not, the boy said. *He's right here!*

I didn't know yet if I believed that heaven was the place all good dead things went to. Or if it was truly where my father and Jacob were. Maybe I just believed in it because it was something the grown-ups told us was true. Maybe when I grew up I'd believe something different. But for now, heaven was as real as our kitchen counters, our living room couch, the oil glistening in the parts in our hair, and I guess that was okay.

I bet he's just really, really tired, the boy said. *I think I'm gonna let him sleep awhile.*

He finally gave up poking and skipped away.

I stared at the dog for a long time. His eyes were only half-closed, and he seemed to be looking off at something. There was such a stillness to him. He was wearing a red collar. I turned it, looking for a number or address, but there wasn't one. Just the name *Spottie* written in black marker.

The hair on the dog's neck felt softer than I had imagined. Beneath it, the skin was still warm.

Ewww, Sage! a kid from the block yelled. *Don't touch him—he might have a disease or something!*

Nothing he can give me now, I said.

Then one of the kids must have pulled the fire alarm.

We could hear the sirens growing closer, and when the fire truck arrived, a ring of us still surrounded Spottie. But the firefighters just shook their heads and got back on their truck. *We can't help you with this,* they said.

As the fire truck pulled off, we all stood around for a while, not sure what to do next. Then, slowly, we headed off in different directions.

I went home because even though I had been on punishment forever, it was feeling like a lot, being outside with the dog thing and all. I climbed back onto my kitchen window seat. A few cats crisscrossed the backyards, but otherwise they were empty. I picked up my latest book, leaned back, and started reading.

That night, I heard a kid tried to set the dead dog on fire.

50

I AVOIDED KNICKERBOCKER AVENUE THE next day because what was left of Spottie was still there. Maybe that kid had thought Spottie would burn to ash and be easily swept away. But he didn't burn to ash. In the summer heat, the block smelled like smoke and burnt hair and something else I couldn't recognize, so I called the thing I didn't know *Spottie* and held my nose to walk down the block.

I worried about Spottie's owner and tried not to wonder if there was a little boy somewhere holding a leash and calling Spottie's name. I tried not to think about how Spottie had once been alive, running after sticks, gobbling up dog food, and barking at strange noises in the night. Tried not to think that he had once been a puppy with tiny puppy teeth and a sweet puppy smell.

A day or two later, Animal Protection finally arrived in a white truck with two men wearing gloves and masks.

As a bunch of people from the block crowded by the factory, some of the grown-ups held handkerchiefs to their faces. The men lifted the dog onto a tarp that they folded around him. Then they put him into the back of their truck and drove away.

A few minutes later, the street cleaner came down Knickerbocker spraying bleach-scented water over the place where Spottie had been.

51

FREDDY CAME BY THE NEXT day with his basketball. *I heard you finally got set free.*

I nodded and moved a step closer to him. I'd missed him.

Yep. Finally. Where you been?

In the Bronx, Freddy said. *Visiting my cousins.*

You hear about the dog that got hit? I asked.

Yeah. I missed that whole thing, but I'm hoping dogs have nine lives. Like cats do.

I hope we all have a whole lotta lives, I said. *And we just keep coming back and living them.*

Jacob too?

Jacob, you, me. Everybody.

I loved that kid, Freddy said. *You know what he said to me once? He said "You got a good heart, Freddy."*

Freddy looked at me. *He said it like he was already some little old man.*

We got quiet for a while, and then Freddy said, *I pass by those flowers and that picture of him and I still can't believe it, you know?*

Yeah. Me neither.

I still see him spinning.

I thought about what Angie had said about Jacob.

Cuz he's out there, I said. *Still flying.*

Yeah, Freddy said.

We got quiet again. When Freddy finally spoke, his voice was soft, unsure, like he was afraid to ask me. *You ever playing ball again, Sage? Ain't the same, you know . . . without you playing.*

I know.

The night before, I'd lain in bed thinking about Jacob, about how quickly time went by. And I'd been thinking about my daddy's smile. Maybe it was because my mother talked about it so much, but I saw it again—in my head. And he was smiling because he was watching me play ball. I was thinking that's the kind of girl I am. The kind that could make my daddy smile just by throwing a ball through a hoop. The kind that could sink that ball again and again and again. I thought about how my daddy's ball was part of the *once was* now. But I wasn't. Not yet.

I need new sneakers first, I said.

For real?! You gonna play again?

I had gotten up from all that thinking and pulled my basketball shoes from my closet. They were moldy and still damp from when I had thrown them in there. I wasn't planning to put them on. Just wanted to look at them. Remember the game.

I'm thinking on it, Freddy.

Don't know why you stopped, anyway.

Somebody said I think I'm a dude. Said "What kind of girl are you?"

Huh? What're you talking about? Who's asking you such a dumb question?

I shrugged. *Nobody.*

You're the Sage kind, Freddy said. *The Sage kind loves ball.*

I smiled. *The Sage kind.* I liked that.

See—I got you smiling, Freddy said. *So, you coming back to the park? I need your jump shot.*

Told you, I said, *I'm thinking on it. Thinking on it real hard.*

Well, think on it harder, cuz I'm tired of getting beat by brothers who don't even ball good. It's embarrassing. Just think hard cuz—

Freddy! I get it!

Okay. Okay.

He zipped his fingers across his lips. But everything he wanted to beg for was right there in his eyes.

52

NEW CURTAINS HUNG FROM OUR bathroom door, and the toilet paper roll had been moved far away from them. The fire felt like a long time ago, but still, at the edges of the door, spots of blackened wood fanned up, while the paint that was once ivory had dried brown and melting.

My mother said she would leave it that way. *I want you to look up every time you're in here,* she said, *and remember what you almost did.*

And every time I looked, I remembered.

Each morning I woke to the sound of my mother's typewriter. I had realized over the summer that there were days she forgot to eat, so I began surprising her in the morning with trays of coffee, buttered toast, scrambled eggs. Some mornings I'd get up early and run to the bakery three blocks from our house and add cinnamon rolls to the tray. We'd sit together eating quietly, my mother reading over her typed pages as she ate, me on the couch opposite her breaking off small pieces of my cinnamon roll and chewing slowly to make it last. There was a tree just outside the window of her office. Over the summer, swallows had built a nest in it, and I listened to them singing as they disappeared into the leaves.

The hollow feeling stayed with me but felt different somehow. Always, there was the ache of something *leaving me*, but some days that ache was more bittersweet than sad. It felt as though . . . as though I was saying goodbye to something that *needed* to go, that I couldn't . . . hold on to anymore. I wanted to ask my mother what this thing was but was terrified she wouldn't know what I was talking about. I knew if that happened, I'd feel lonelier than I ever had before.

When we finished our breakfast, my mother hugged me, hard.

I knew she had forgiven me for the fire. But each time she hugged me, I felt her forgiveness all over again. I felt that bathroom door swinging open and her on the other side. I felt the fresh air after the smoke and the cool after the heat.

53

I KEPT THINKING ABOUT TIME. How quickly it moved. How slowly it moved. How the school year dragged on and on and the summer blurred by us. How my mother sometimes forgot time and said *Did that happen yesterday or the day before?*

Shelly, who lived across the street, had a baby girl. She named the baby Ivy Lee and dressed her up in pinks, pale yellows, and deep greens. When she brought her outside, she checked our hands for dirt before letting us touch the baby. Ivy Lee was so new and perfect and brown and beautiful that I felt a heaviness rise up in my throat. My mother was there beside me and I hugged her, pressing my face into her blouse.

Was I ever that little and perfect? I asked.

And my mother smiled and said *You still are perfect.*

But time moves on . . .

Shelly's baby must be long past crawling—walking and counting now. Some days I wonder if I'd recognize her on the street. Were her cheeks still round or had they sharpened? Was her hair still a cap of tight curls or had she straightened it? And the dimples on the back of her chubby hands, did they remain?

I thought about how babies don't understand time. It moves around them without their knowing until one day they're in school and a teacher brings a clock into the room and says *Today we're going to learn how to tell time.*

Before we learn to tell time, time doesn't matter at all.

54

SOME DAYS, WHEN FREDDY CAME over, we put records on the record player and placed the needle down to make them play. We couldn't afford whole record albums, so we settled for the single songs on the 45s, pulling them from paper sleeves and trying to only touch the edges so we didn't scratch them. If there was a scratch on the record, the needle skipped and parts of the song repeated themselves. Michael Jackson said *A, B— A, B— A, B— A, B—* until our ears hurt. Donny Osmond said *One bad— One bad— One bad—* until we hated the song. *Don't scratch the record,* we warned. But somehow it always happened. And when it did, we took the ruined records outside and flung them like Frisbees into the street. We made wishes that would only come true if the records landed A-side up. But too often, they landed with the B side showing. And the B side was the wrong side. The B side was the song no one ever walked into the record store to buy. On a full album, it was the song that you often lifted the needle up to skip over.

Before they landed, though, our records sailed through the air like silent black songs. If you squinted and held your ears, you could bring the music back again. *A, B, C / Easy as 1, 2, 3* and *One bad apple don't spoil the whole bunch, girl* ringing low and clear through the hot summer breeze.

55

IT WAS DURING THAT SUMMER, too, that a song coming from a teenager's radio caught my ears off guard. My heart followed. A man whose voice sounded like tears was singing about California dreaming. I broke away from my handball game and moved closer to the sound.

Who is that?

José Feliciano, the teenager said. *How come you don't know that?*

I shrugged.

He's blind, the teenager said. *And he plays guitar.*

I stood there imagining the singer, his open eyes like closed ones, feeling the music on his guitar with his fingers. When he sang *I went for a walk on a winter's day,* it sounded like prayer. A prayer I wanted to always hold inside of me. A prayer for a whole world nobody else had ever seen. I wanted to walk all the way to California. I wanted, suddenly, for the hot sun to melt into winter snow.

Look at her, the teenager said to nobody. *She's in a trance.*

The song ended, and even though the streetlights hadn't yet come on, it didn't feel like there was anything else really left to the day. I walked down the block to my building. Pushed open the door. And went inside to count out the allowance I had saved.

I bought José Feliciano's record, with a song called "Light My Fire" on the B side. *If that song's going to have you messing with matches again . . .* my mother said. I told her I only bought the record to dream about California. I told her José was blind. *He's a grown man,* my mother said. *Don't call him by his first name like he's one of your little friends.*

But he *was* a friend. Freddy came over for dinner, and afterward, we sat in the living room beside the record player, returning the needle to the beginning of the song when the record ended. *All the leaves are brown,* we sang along with Mr. Feliciano. *And the sky is gray.*

This guy, man, Freddy said. *His voice . . . it's so real, right?*

Outside, the summer sun sunk to bright gold, then orange. Then gone. The streetlights came on. In the distance, always, there was the sound of a fire truck. There was also the sound of children playing. And somewhere in the near darkness, I could hear Mr. Jolly singing, his voice deep and clear. The fires, like the summer sun and the leaves of autumn, would continue to burn—bright orange and red and gold. There were the fires, yes. But there was so much beauty too.

56

FREDDY, I SAID. *CAN I tell you something?*

Freddy looked at me. *Sure.*

This guy in the park . . . I was playing basketball by myself one day, and this guy— I stopped speaking as quickly as I had started.

What, Sage? Did somebody hurt you?! I'll find him, I swear! And I'll—

He just . . .

I told Freddy the whole story. How close the guy got to me. What he said. How he stole my ball. How scared I had been.

Freddy got quiet for a long time. The record had come to the end and was just spinning beneath the needle, making a scratchy sound.

That's not right, Freddy said. *I bet he was jealous, is all.*

I don't know, Freddy. He was so . . . so mad *at me.*

Well, you ever seen yourself play, Sage? Sometimes I even get mad at how good you are. Your layup is crazy! But seriously, that was messed up what he did to you. I'm sorry.

I put the needle back to the beginning of the song. Something felt lifted off of me. Something heavy and hard was gone.

So that's why you stopped playing?

I nodded. *I know it's stupid, but it's like he scared the game out of me. And then he took my ball.*

Nah, Sage. You can't let him do that. What if one day the Knicks recruit girls, and then you haven't been playing, so you ain't even got a dream anymore?

I'm the only one who believes that's gonna happen, I said.

But what if it does?

You think I'm not . . . a real girl? Like the other girls on the block?

Nah, Freddy said. *That's stupid. I mean, you're not stupid. But that's stupid. Just cuz you the only girl on that court. Just cuz you can play ball. You still got a braid and—*

Freddy looked embarrassed.

Other stuff, he said. *I just hope you come back.*

I will, I said.

You never let what people say bother you before, Sage. And plus, you got the ball inside of you. Nobody can steal that.

I know, I said. *They can't.*

I turned the volume up. Freddy started singing along to the record. After a minute, so did I.

57

MY MOM BOUGHT ME A new pair of white All Stars with black laces. The next morning, I laced them up and grabbed the basketball from my dresser. Memories washed over me—a smooth layup, the sweet spin of the ball as it sailed through the air, the way it felt inside my chest when I scored. But the new ball felt weird in my hands, and my sneakers weren't broken in. I could feel the new cut of them against the sides of my feet as I ran to meet Freddy.

She's back! Freddy said the minute I walked into the park. He ran over to me and grabbed my ball.

It needs air, he said, bouncing it. *It hardly even bounces.*

I don't have a pump, I said. *Randy's the pump dude.*

We can use my ball, Randy said. *I'll bring my pump tomorrow for yours. Hopefully the needle's not broke.*

I took a quick look around the park. It was crowded with kids playing on the field and teenagers playing music. If that guy was around, I didn't see him. Strangely, a part of me wanted to. I wanted him to show up on the court with all my friends around me. I wanted him to grab my ball. I was ready this time. He had taken something from me, and I was ready to take it back.

I got Sage, Randy said.

Freddy threw up his hands. *Dang, Randy,* he said. *I wanted Sage.*

Too slow, brother, Randy said. *You not the only one been waiting for her to get back here.*

There were two other guys standing against the fence waiting to play. Freddy chose one of them and we started the game.

It felt easy and right and good to be playing ball again.

I don't know if Freddy had told them anything, but everybody acted like it was just another day in the park. And all of us, including me, were right where we belonged.

58

ON ONE OF THE LAST days of summer, my mother woke me in the early morning.

I have a surprise, Sage, she said, her weight at the foot of my bed. *We're moving.*

I pulled the comforter with its pattern of basketballs over my head. I was still half-asleep. Maybe I was dreaming.

Wake up, my mother said. I heard something jangling. *I finally bought us a house made of brick.*

I peeked out. The jangling sound was keys. My mother held them above me, smiling. *I signed the paperwork yesterday.*

Huh? For real? I don't want to leave here . . . How far away is it? Brick?

I didn't know one body could have so many feelings inside it at the same time—excitement and heartbreak and fear. I pulled the covers back over my head like a shield.

59

HOW FAR AWAY? FREDDY ASKED. *And why didn't you tell me?*

I didn't know it was gonna happen so soon. I mean—I knew my mom's been saving to move for a long time, but I didn't believe that it would ever really happen . . .

I stopped suddenly, the news of it all sinking in.

We were sitting on the ground beneath the rim of the basketball hoop.

Sage?

Huh?

You didn't say how far away . . .

Sorry. I was thinking.

About what?

I shrugged. *It's in Queens.*

Where in Queens?

It's called Hollis. No so far. You take a train and then a bus.

I'm not allowed to take the train by myself.

Freddy took the ball from me and started dribbling it fast and close to the ground. He was looking at it, but I could tell his face was fighting something.

When? he said to the ball.

Moving truck coming Sunday morning.

Whoa, that's so soon. Freddy kept dribbling. Harder and faster. But still not looking at me. I put my hand on the ball and pressed it to the ground.

We'll be back, I said. *For visiting. It's not like we're never gonna hang out again, right?*

I guess. You still got my number?

I recited his number to him.

Yup, that's it.

You still have mine?

Yeah, he said.

But you don't know it by heart.

Freddy stood up, dribbled the ball out to the foul line.

I do. Just don't want to say it, that's all.

Say it, I said.

I walked over to the foul line and tried to take the ball. But Freddy dribbled it away, took a layup. And missed.

If I say it, it'll mean you're really moving away from here.

We looked at each other for a long time.

Gonna miss you, Slick, he said quietly. *You gonna remember me?*

I'm not moving to the moon, Slick. Just Queens.

I took the shot from the outside line, rolling it off my fingers and into the air. Me and Freddy watched it. Watched the ball sail toward the sky like it could fly forever. Like time wouldn't turn the ball and the game and this moment with me and Freddy to ash. The ball kept flying. And maybe somewhere out there in time, it's flying still.

60

THE BLOCK CAME OUT TO say goodbye.

Mr. Jolly and lots of the neighborhood kids. Angie and her sister and her parents. Mrs. Peat, in her church dress and hat, handed me a gift-wrapped Bible and gave me a hug. Randy came by too. He would be leaving for boarding school the next day and was already wearing a T-shirt with the name of his new school across the front. When he handed me a pair of tube socks with the Knicks' colors ringing them, I wanted to hug him hard and hide my tears in his neck.

Me and some of the dudes went in on these, he said, handing them to me. But I held myself together, wiping my eyes and giving him a quick hug, before slapping his hand the way we'd always done.

Samara brought us some butter-and-jelly biscuits her mother had made. Shelly brought Ivy Lee over and let me hold her one more time, her sleeping head resting on my shoulder. And the family that had just moved into the apartment above them across the street waved from their stoop.

Mama leaned over to me and whispered *I see Freddy slinking at the corner. Maybe you need to say goodbye to him again.*

I looked over in time to see Freddy duck behind the factory wall, handed Ivy Lee back to Shelly, and sprinted toward him.

Don't get lost, Sage, my mother said just as I turned the corner.

Hey, I said to Freddy.

He had squatted down against the factory building.

I was gonna put this in your mailbox, he said, holding out a wad of tissue. *Didn't know there'd be so many people all around y'all like that, though.*

I looked at the wad of tissue.

You saying my nose is runny or something?

It's not just tissue-tissue. Man, just open it!

I unballed the tissues. There was a basketball needle inside.

I couldn't afford to buy the whole pump, Freddy said. *But everybody always be needing one of these, right?*

My eyes got blurry and I used the wadded tissue to wipe at them.

Yeah, I said, barely able to choke it out. *Thanks, Freddy.*

You're gonna keep playing ball, right, Sage?

I nodded.

I bet you could do it.

Do what?

Make it to the NBA. You're good. Really good.

Without even thinking, I hugged Freddy, holding on to him. I felt his arm wrap around and hug me back. We stood like that for I don't know how long, but when we pulled away, we didn't look at each other. Freddy looked down at the ground and I stared at my basketball needle.

Thanks, Freddy.

Anytime.

My mother called me.

I gotta go, I said.

I know.

You think the Knicks got a chance this year?

Freddy shrugged. *Holzman thinks so, and he's the coach, so . . .*

That'd be cool.

Yeah, Freddy said. *It would be.*

Gonna miss you, Slick, I said.

Gonna miss you, Slick, Freddy said back.

My mother called for me again.

But me and Freddy just stood there together. For how long, I don't even remember now.

61

OUR NEW HOUSE STOOD ALONE in the middle of a block lined with trees. The door was painted bright red and had a small knocker hanging from the center of it.

And the house was made of brick.

As our car pulled up to it, a bunny ran across the front lawn and disappeared behind the house. By the time the moving van pulled up a few minutes later, I had already run around to the back in search of it. The backyard had a narrow stone path leading to a picnic table and chairs. There were flowers growing along the edges of the yard and plants in more shades of green than I had ever seen.

Even though it was only the beginning of September, leaves had started falling from the tree near the house, and they sprinkled the ground with bright yellow. I stood there, staring up at the tree. A soft wind blew, trembling the leaves. I thought of Freddy leaning out of his high-up window that first day I met him, and something caught me.

Bushwick was so far away from here. Freddy was so far away. And we had this now—a brick house with a tree in the backyard. A bunny that felt safe enough to run free. Birds—so many birds—singing in the trees. It wasn't fair. Freddy should have this too. And Jacob should have had it. And all of the families my mother had brought water and blankets and clothing to—they should have this . . .

I didn't know when my mother had come up behind me.

We did it, Sage, she said softly. I turned toward her.

I miss Freddy, I said.

And standing in that stunning yard, with flowers and leaves and birds and a tree and a bunny somewhere close, maybe, but hiding, sadness pushed the beauty of this place back like a curtain.

I want to go home, I whispered.

This is home now, my mother said. She pulled me to her. Pressed her cheek against the top of my head. I wrapped my arms around her waist. We stood there like that for a long time. Just holding on.

62

THERE ARE EMPTY SPACES IN memory. Long days like blank pages. I don't remember the names of the books I read that year. I don't remember Freddy's mother's name or the house Randy lived in on Cornelia Street. I do remember the men delivering our first color TV in a box that we watched the kids on the block play inside of until it was no more than brown shreds of cardboard scattered along the street. And I remember my mother sending me out to clean it up and how Freddy appeared there, beside me, bending with me. *The sooner we get this done, the sooner we can get to the park,* he said. How clearly his words ring back through time.

And I remember the boy in the park, his words erasing me for weeks. *What kind of girl are you?* I remember my ball disappearing. My basketball shoes growing moldy in the back of my closet. The hollow place his words left behind.

But now even that has faded.

And maybe that's what matters. That time soothes the sharp sting of pain. Until only the soft and hazy edges of the hurt are remembered.

63

AUTUMN CAME AND SCHOOL BEGAN again. A different school in a redbrick building with a full court in the gym and a soccer field outside.

The building was new and so were many of the kids inside it. Our families had all moved from places like East New York, the South Bronx, Bushwick, and Brownsville. And once again the *Daily News* had something to say about it, reporting about how families like ours *had run from impoverished neighborhoods* to places in Queens like Laurelton, Cambria Heights, Springfield Gardens, and Hollis.

But they weren't *impoverished neighborhoods*. They were places we had called *home*.

And we hadn't run from *home*. We had run from fires in Bushwick and tenement buildings where landlords disappeared in Brownsville. We had run from paint peeling from walls and plaster crumbling from ceilings in the Bronx. From broken windows stuffed with plastic in the wintertime and mice peeking through holes in wooden floors in East New York. I didn't know that all over the city, parents had spent years putting money in jars and envelopes. That they had wanted lawns and backyards and parks with rolling hills. They had wanted quiet streets and good schools. And brick houses.

They had wanted *evergreen*.

We were their children. Again and again they said *We want the best for you.*

So we showed up on that first day of school in new clothes and freshly washed hair. We looked around at each other and thought about the friends we'd left behind. I searched faces and wondered if I'd find somebody like Freddy ever again.

64

ON THAT FIRST DAY OF school, a girl named Lisa sat behind me. One of her eyes was bigger than the other and was a startling blue.

It's glass, Lisa told the group of kids that gathered around her asking questions. *I lost that eye in an accident.*

There were small groups of kids who already knew each other. I walked through the halls watching them bump shoulders as they walked to their classes together. But most of us were new to the school and a little bit afraid.

At lunch, the kids who knew each other put their book bags and jackets on the seats beside and across from their own. When any of us new kids approached, they said *Taken, newbie!* and smirked, waiting for us to argue. But we didn't. We stood looking lost as we gripped our trays of peanut butter sandwiches, cartons of chocolate milk, and paper cups of cling peaches.

So many of us didn't know *anyone*. So we became a "we" of outside kids, new and unsure and sometimes mean. And our meanness always found Lisa, alone at a lunch table, alone in the schoolyard, alone in the hallway.

We said *Take your eye out!*

But Lisa just looked at us through two different-colored eyes.

We said *You're not like the rest of us!*

We laughed. We pointed. And sometimes we ran away. Because we didn't know that there wasn't a *rest of us* yet. That all of us were going to be a Lisa sometimes.

In the late afternoon, when the glass eye grew as heavy and painful as the names we called her, Lisa cupped her hand over it, releasing it from its too-tight socket. Then, quiet as breath and stunningly alone, Lisa did what so many of us wished we had the courage to do—she put her head down on her desk and wept.

65

ONE SATURDAY, MY MOTHER AND I took a bus and then a train to Coney Island. I had hoped that Freddy could meet us there, but he was in the Bronx with his cousins.

The day was bright and on the edge of being cold. As we ate hot dogs on the boardwalk, we huddled close to each other for warmth and looked out at the ocean. Seagulls swooped down for scraps of pizza and sanded-over fries while, behind us, the Ferris wheel spun a few screaming riders above the earth and a roller coaster made of wood rumbled. In the distance, I could hear a siren.

I knew I'd miss Freddy, I said to my mother. *But I never thought I'd miss the sound of sirens. It's so quiet in Hollis.*

You'll see him again, my mother said. *We're not that far away.*

We stared out at the ocean for a while.

Strange, my mother said finally. *I feel like I still hear the sirens in Queens. The ghosts of them.*

You don't believe in ghosts, Ma.

I believe in memory, though. Memory's like a ghost.

Maybe, I said. *It's just all so . . . so weird. I didn't know I'd miss* everything, *you know. Stuff like just walking out of our house every day and seeing friends—people who know us.*

A huge wave broke white against the shore, then foamed quietly back into the ocean.

My mother pulled me closer, kissed the top of my head.

You'll see them again, Sage. And you'll make lots of friends and memories. You have years and years, my love.

But it'll be different, I said. *I'll be different and they'll be different. And my memories are already disappearing.*

Try to find a way to hold on to them, then. Try to remember a little something every day.

We finished our hot dogs and walked down to the edge of the water, the wind and bits of sand blowing against our faces.

I crouched down and wrote a sentence in the sand.

Remember the fires. Remember Freddy. Remember Bushwick. Always.

The tide was rising and the waves crawled up the hill of the shore, then ebbed away with my words.

You have to write it somewhere more permanent, my mother said.

You're the writer, Ma.

My mother smiled.

Maybe you're a writer too.

66

HEY, SAGE.

Hey, Slick.

Whatchu doing?

I was watching the game, but now I'm talking to you on the phone. You?

Same.

You still think the Knicks gonna take it this year?

Maybe, Freddy said. *They still got Earl the Pearl.*

And Walt Frazier.

Still mad I missed going to Coney Island with you—maybe another time. When you coming back this way?

I was gonna come last Sunday, I said, *but my mother got a cold.*

Maybe next week?

Maybe. There's two bluebirds in my backyard. And a bunny lives there too.

For real? Freddy said.

Yup.

That's cool. Oh shoot! You see he missed that easy pass? Let me go watch this game before they lose again.

Me too, I said.

Bye, Slick.

Bye, Slick.

67

ONE MORNING, I GOT TO school long before the first bell rang, hoping to finish a science project that was due that afternoon. Lisa was at the basketball court wearing black All Stars and shooting baskets by herself. I stood a bit away watching her. She kept shooting, sinking shot after shot after shot.

Lisa, I called. She jumped, and I realized I had been standing on the side where she couldn't see—the side where she had the glass eye.

She turned and looked at me, then went back to shooting without saying anything.

Hey, I said.

Hey, yourself.

I didn't know you played basketball.

Lisa kept shooting without saying anything.

I said, I didn't . . .

I heard you, Lisa said.

She stopped shooting finally and looked at me.

What about it, she finally said.

I just . . . I just didn't know, is all.

Well, I do, she said. She went over to the rim and stuffed the ball into a huge tote bag that was sitting beside her book bag, then grabbed both bags and started heading toward the school. But after a few steps, she stopped and looked at me.

It was a mistake, she said.

I just stood there, confused.

My eye. It was supposed to be brown, not blue. They made a mistake. But now we have to wait until I outgrow this one before I can get the next one. Because the government paid for it and you get what you get.

She started walking again. Then turned back to me.

Where did you move here from? she asked.

Brooklyn.

I moved from the Bronx.

We looked at each other.

Because of fire? I asked.

Lisa nodded slowly. *We got burnt out,* she said. *You?*

No, I said. *But the fires were getting way too close.*

68

THE NEXT MORNING, I WAS at the school basketball court before Lisa got there, working on my outside shot. She showed up a few minutes later and watched me from the schoolyard entrance for a long time before coming closer. My shot was off that morning, hitting the rim again and again. The rim here was upright with a chain-link net. In Bushwick, the rim had been bent from years and years of balls bouncing off of it and teenagers grabbing on to it.

You're not hooking your wrist enough, Lisa finally said, coming closer.

Yeah I am. I took another shot and missed again, grabbed the ball and laid it up. *The rim is different here.*

It's just a rim. Lisa held her hands out for me to throw her the ball. I rolled my eyes but passed it to her. She took a few steps out and easily sank a jumper, her wrist flicking deep.

Now you, she said.

I jogged out next to her and took the same shot, bending my wrist a little more and watching the ball sail into the basket.

Sweet, Lisa said. *Everyplace you go, the rim is always a little bit different. So, like, what you did where you used to play might not work in the next place.*

I had grabbed the ball and moved farther from the basket. Lisa watched me take the shot, bending my wrist deeper than I'd ever had to bend it. It felt strange. But when the ball sank into the basket and the chain link jingled like music, it felt good.

Where'd you learn ball? I asked Lisa. We moved in closer to the basket, taking turns shooting. Her dribble was smoother than anything I'd ever seen.

Lisa shrugged. *I have five brothers. They're all older than me, and my mom always made them take me to the park.*

She took a shot and missed. I grabbed the rebound and laid it up.

I could either sit there and watch them play or get in the game. She looked at me and smiled. *I can beat all of them now. You?*

My dad, I said.

Can you beat him now?

He died.

Lisa had the ball. She didn't shoot it, though. Just froze and looked at me.

But if he was still living, she finally said. *You think you could beat him?*

69

IF SOMEONE HAD BEEN THERE to take a picture of us those next few mornings, it would have been me and Lisa on that court.

Me and Lisa, dribbling, laughing, standing at the foul line.

The sun rising above the rim.

And always there would be the ball—sailing through the air.

70

Do You Like to Play Basketball?
Are You a Girl?
Come to the Outside Court
Tuesday 3:30 Sharp
Look for Sage
(I'm tall. I have a braid.)

71

THAT TUESDAY, I GOT TO the basketball court at 3:15. It was drizzling but the afternoon was warm, and it wasn't enough rain to make the ball slippery. Still, I was the only one on the court. I kept checking for Lisa, who had promised she'd show up. But there was no sign of her, so I practiced my layup—left side, then right, my weaker side— and worked the backboard, hoping the thud of the ball against it would drown out the sinking feeling. The sign I'd posted outside the girls' bathroom was still there. Someone had ripped off a tiny corner of it, but otherwise no one had bothered it.

Maybe this was a dumb idea.

Hey.

I turned from shooting. Lisa was standing there.

Hey.

I threw her the ball and she started dribbling smooth as water.

Your ball needs air, she said.

I know. I got a needle, but I don't have a pump.

I'll bring my pump tomorrow.

The side door opened and three girls I had seen around school headed toward the basketball court.

Y'all putting together a game? the tallest one asked. She held her hands apart, and Lisa passed her the ball. *I didn't even know there were other girls who played,* she said. *That's tight!*

She shot the ball and missed. *All good. I gotta warm up,* she said.

A car pulled up just outside the schoolyard gate, and the twins who were in the eighth grade jumped out and waved to the driver, then ran over.

Y'all started already? one of them asked.

Can you give it five minutes? the other one said. *We got three other friends coming. You Sage?*

I nodded, and it felt like everyone was talking at once. About ball, about girls playing. About jealous guys. About the Knicks and the Philadelphia 76ers and basketball sneakers.

Lisa took a shot and the ball sailed in so smoothly, everyone fell quiet for a minute.

The tall girl, whose name was Bea, said *You got game, girl!*

I know, Lisa said.

The three girls we'd been waiting on finally walked up just as the drizzle was ending.

Let's choose up sides, I said. *I got Lisa.*

Bea called for one of the twins, and in a few minutes we had two teams throwing the ball around and shooting.

So what's this gonna be, Sage? Bea asked as we warmed up.

I don't know, I said. *Whatever we want it to be.*

I like that, Bea said. *We're inventing this new kinda thing.*

We played until the streetlights came on.

72

IT MUST HAVE BEEN ABOUT a year before my mother and I went back to the old neighborhood. When we returned, it felt different, even as neighbors poured out of their houses to hug us and tell me how tall I'd gotten.

What are you now, Mr. Jolly asked, *close to six feet?*

Five eight, I said.

Isn't that something. Mr. Jolly grinned. *You might end up playing professional basketball after all.*

Two houses on our block had burned, and another had been taken over by the city—its windows and doors boarded with wood.

On Palmetto, Freddy's building was the only one standing, but he, too, couldn't be found. By then, the calls from Freddy had pretty much stopped coming. A missed call to me, a missed call to him. Freddy running out to shoot hoops but promising to call me back and forgetting. The same from me. Spending the weekend playing ball and then school on Monday and then something else.

So much time had passed, and now here I was staring at a block that no longer felt like home. Until a siren grew closer, familiar as breath.

A siren—all that remained of home.

73

THE OLD NEIGHBORHOOD FADED AS the new one became *home*.

We named our group of girl ballplayers the Hollis Hoopers and played ball every chance we got. Boys started coming over, asking to play against us. We whupped them every single time.

Somewhere over all that ball and walking scared through seventh grade and getting used to the silence of a brick house with a bunny in the backyard, Lisa and I became friends. I learned where to stand so that she could always know I was there and how to look into the eye that could see me. The bright blue of her glass eye faded into just *Lisa's eye*, another part of who my friend was—a part of her she didn't have to explain.

And seventh grade got more familiar. And we got less afraid. And maybe, I hope, kinder.

74

SO MUCH OF IT IS gone now. Maybe not exactly gone, but *different* from the way it was back then. Back before we learned that some landlords were setting their own buildings on fire to collect insurance money.

So many houses, like the trees that had once filled a forest there, were part of the *once was* now.

The small children gathering on stoops to *eeny-meeny-miny-moe* a leader are just a memory's ghost now. Their untied sneakers. Their cutoff shorts and yellowing T-shirts. Their bodies angling over mattresses. The ices they shared that melted blue and red down their wrists and arms. The treeless sidewalk stained for always from the one time a little boy cracked an egg on it, losing a nickel to a friend when it didn't fry. Gone.

Now you see it.

Now you don't.

And Freddy too.

His family moved to Queens, someone said. *Or Long Island.*

They bought a house, someone said. *He has a pool in his back-yard.*

And even if it isn't true, I like to think they made it out of here. They made it home.

75

I AM WONDERING NOW: WHO else remembers that year of fires?

Who else remembers the Bushwick we once lived in?

Who else remembers us?

76

FOR A LONG TIME, I looked for Freddy in the faces of the boys walking through Queens. In each new classroom and the wide aisles of the grocery stores. I looked for him on the basketball courts and in the audiences of the Knicks games I watched on television.

And when Smokey the Bear came on the screen and looked at me, I thought of Freddy hanging out of his window on a block that would soon burn to the ground.

Hey, girl! Where's the park at?

I didn't know that, years and years later, I would run into Freddy near where his family lived in a stone building across from Central Park. He would be taller than me and his afro would be gone. But his eyes would be the same. And his smile. And we would grab each other like we had no plans of ever letting go, laughing and crying and laughing some more. And we'd walk to a café, where we ordered hot chocolate and beignets. Where the minutes faded into hours and the years melted away.

77

I CAN'T BELIEVE YOU'RE MOVING away from here, Freddy had said to me that day he found out we were leaving Bushwick.

If you could live anywhere, I asked him, *where would you want to be?*

I remember it was almost dark out. The streetlights had come on. Little kids ran up and down the sidewalk, yelling and laughing. Soon, mothers would come to the windows and call them inside. But for now, they were happy. For once, there were no other sounds. Not the sounds of car horns. Not the sounds of sirens. Not even the music of an ice cream truck. Just the children's laughter. So much of it. Everywhere.

Here, he said. *But I'd want it to be different.*

Different how?

Not always burning. I wish the houses could all stay standing like the ones on Ridgewood Place. For always.

We stopped walking and he looked at me. *You know why?*

Cuz no one wants their house to burn?

Because if the houses stayed standing for always, then you wouldn't be moving away and I'd always be here and you and me would always be shooting hoops or walking down this block and the kids here would always be playing. If there's no Palmetto Street, there isn't any of this stuff.

We got to the corner and looked up at Freddy's windows. White curtains blew in and out. Behind them, we could see the golden glow of his living room lights. Just above his building, the moon was full and white and still.

You ever miss something that's right there in front of you, Sage?

Yeah, I said, and I could feel tears starting.

Because I had finally come to understand the hollowness in my chest. All year, I had already been missing all of this, even though it was right in front of me. Right in front of me but, building by building, burning away. When I finally asked my mother about it, she said *That's what growing up feels like.*

While Freddy and I stood there, I looked up at his window and could see the year passing. There was Freddy calling out to me. There was his mother, with her bag of Avon, spraying perfume onto my mother's wrist. And his cousins were there, all of us dancing to the O'Jays. And Jacob was there too. *Hey, Freddy! Sage! Watch me!* There was the world I had known so well the year I was twelve, already fading.

You know what makes me really, really sad, Sage? Freddy said.

I took a deep breath, fighting back tears again.

When I left earlier, he said, *my mom was starting to make beignets. I'm just thinking about the future, when I'm gonna have to find someone new to share them with.*

Freddy looked at me, then grinned and said, *But that's not today!* He started running up his stoop. But I was faster and pushed ahead of him, taking the stairs two at a time. The smell of sugar filled the hallway, and I could hear his mother singing along to a new José Feliciano song.

And even though I knew in that moment that one day his

building would be gone, for now there was music playing. For now there was me and Freddy out of breath and laughing. For now, just inside his apartment door, all the sweetness in the world was waiting.

And that sweetness would remain with me. And with Freddy.

Always.

THE END

ABOUT THE MATCHBOX

ALTHOUGH THIS BOOK IS FICTION, it's based on a real time and place.

When I was growing up in the Bushwick section of Brooklyn in the 1970s and '80s, the papers *did* call my neighborhood "The Matchbox" because there were so many fires. We knew people who had lost their homes to fire, and my family worried about our own house going up in flames. Because the houses were connected, if one house burned, chances were the houses on either side of it would also be damaged or destroyed by fire. As children we watched, fascinated, as firefighters fought blazes that seemed unbeatable. And days after the fire, kids could be seen searching the wreckage for "treasures."

Somehow, our block was spared, and decades later, the houses on the block I grew up on remain standing. Palmetto Street wasn't as lucky. By the time I left for college, most of the block that Freddy's family lived on had burned to the ground.

But the world turns upside down. Then rights itself again.

If you walk through Bushwick today, it's a different place. The houses on Palmetto Street have been rebuilt, and block after block, the houses stand proudly on tree-lined streets. Sage's basketball courts have been covered in Astroturf and turned into a soccer field.

And Ridgewood Place remains as it always was.

Freddy, Sage, Jacob, Gwen, Shaunessy, Angie, Lisa, and all the other characters in this book were imagined, sketched on the page, filled in a bit more with each rewrite, and finally emerged feeling like real people. I created them to tell a story I've been wanting to tell for a long time and set that story in the 1970s.

The Bushwick of my past is long gone. But in writing this book, I was able to go home again.

—*Jacqueline*

ACKNOWLEDGMENTS

FIRST AND ALWAYS, I THANK the streets of the Bushwick section of Brooklyn, New York, for giving me so many stories to tell. And thank you to the people on those streets who helped raise me to the point where I could tell those stories: The women whose forearms rested on pillows as they leaned out apartment building windows. The men behind bodega counters who knew me by name. The friends who ran those streets with me. The old men cheering us on from their places around folding tables loaded with dominoes. The mothers and fathers coming home from long days of work whose tired smiles reflected their joy and pride in their children's freedom. The abuelitas who were too old to work but not too old to make us coconut ices on hot summer days. Because of all of these grown folks, I am and continue to be so.

Writers write in solitude, until they don't.

So thank you, Sadie Rain, my brilliant librarian niece, who jumped to the task of researching Black firefighters in the

1970s, and Marie E. Cronin, who delivered more information just when I needed it.

Thanks to my family—who suffers through this writing life with grace, amazing meals, Bananagrams, Wordle, laughter, and the occasional roll of the eyes.

Of course, thank you, Nancy Paulsen, for always understanding where I'm trying to go to in a narrative and helping me get there, and Cindy Howle, for catching every repeated word, wrong fact about the Knicks, overuse of ellipses, and so much more.

Thank you, librarians and teachers. I stand with you. Always.